I was crouching down in front of a window that would only open two inches. Two floors below, the wagon was just starting to pull away. I had at most a few seconds before they would be out of pistol range. Maybe six, seven seconds.

It was a big farm wagon, the three thugs sitting down in back, Belden and Evelyn up front.

I decided to take the thugs out first. But did I trust myself to hit them and not hit Evelyn? Gripping the gun, trying to become familiar with it, I squeezed off—one—two—three—

The horses cried and bucked. The three thugs slumped forward. One I got in the face, one I got in the side of the head, one I got in the chest.

Also by Ed Gorman:

NIGHT KILLS
DEATH GROUND
WOLF MOON*

with Martin H. Greenberg:

CAT CRIMES
CAT CRIMES II

*Published by Fawcett Books

THE
SHARPSHOOTER

Ed Gorman

FAWCETT GOLD MEDAL • NEW YORK

A Fawcett Gold Medal Book
Published by Ballantine Books
Copyright © 1993 by Ed Gorman

All rights reserved under International and Pan-American Copyright Conventions. Published in the United States of America by Ballantine Books, a division of Random House, Inc., New York, and simultaneously in Canada by Random House of Canada Limited, Toronto.

Library of Congress Catalog Card Number: 93-90540

ISBN 0-449-14835-1

Manufactured in the United States of America

First Edition: January 1994

To Gail Cross:
One of the most decent people
I've ever known —EG

Prologue

He had killed 46 white men, 27 Negroes, 38 Chinese, 81 Injuns, and 103 snakes of the poisonous variety. He had saved the lives of 106 virgins, 42 elderly ladies, 51 lawmen, and 67 children. He had uncovered 32 secret passages, 44 trapdoors, and 18 hidden alligator pits.

He had done all this before reaching the age of thirty-five and without leaving his New York hotel room very often. And while weighing somewhere between forty and sixty more pounds than he should have.

His name was Chester D. Fulbright and he was a dime novelist whose wares were mostly sold through the Sears Roebuck catalog, along with such other books as Her Desperate Victory by Mrs. Rayne and Her Only Sin by Bertha M. Clay.

He had gone west once, for a month and a half, but he had found the people there to be preposterously uncivilized. And smell? My God, he'd never smelled people like that before.

He was much happier in New York dreaming about the West . . . his Old West . . . not the one he'd found at all his train stops.

Still, the trip hadn't been wasted, because in Idaho—who the hell could remember the name of the godforsaken

1

town?—*a shambling woolly man, most appreciative of the drinks Chester kept buying for everybody, leaned toward Chester and said,* "You wanna hear a story, you bein' an arthor and all?"

"I am always much obliged to hear a true tale of the West," *said Chester in that inimitable way of his.*

"Well, this one'll curl yer hair, young fella, and I mean the hair on every part of your body."

That was another thing about these westerners. Vulgar. Curl the hair on every part of your body, indeed.

But Chester listened, as was only polite, and the shambling woolly man soon had him hooked, just as he had everybody in the suddenly quiet saloon hooked.

"Yessir," *the shambling woolly man said,* " 'twer a day back in 'ninety-four. And I'll tell it to you just the way my friend said it happened to him . . ."

1

The night of the jailbreak, the night of the killing that followed, I was at the roulette table in the Gold Dust Casino.

I was playing, as I played too many nights, with no luck at all. Every few minutes, whiskey getting mean in me, I'd glance down at one of the thick, postlike legs supporting the table and wonder if there were wires inside those legs. Wires that controlled the roulette wheel. It happened a lot more than most folks understood.

The casino man leaned close to me, so the others wouldn't hear, and said, "Hate to tell you this, Mr. Coldwell, but you're out of credit."

"Bullshit," I said. I could hear how drunk and angry I was getting.

"C'mon, now, you don't want to get us both in trouble, do you, Mr. Coldwell?"

He took gentle hold of my shirtsleeve. I jerked the sleeve away.

By now, the other four men at the table were watching us. I saw one of them wink to another. In a town like this, everybody knew your story. There were no secrets. The wink earned a smirk. I seemed to attract a lot of smirks these days.

3

"I'd call Mr. Belden, I surely would," the casino man said, "but—well, this ain't the night to walk up them stairs and get him. If you know what I mean."

He nodded to the north wall and the staircase leading to the second and third floors. The dance girls and the outright whores lived on the second. Jeremiah Belden had a fancy apartment on the third.

Belden was my boss, having bought the Wild West show I owned when I'd been unable to pay my gambling debt to him. Belden City had been owned by Jeremiah Belden's father when it was still a gold strike town of tent cities and six different graveyards. Jeremiah had civilized it some by disguising his greed with what he called "family places." There were now three churches, a hospital, a town hall, a city park, and the remnants of my Wild West show, which was now called "The Belden Family Wild West Spectacular." Of course, he still prospered from the Gold Dust Casino, which brought miners and farmers and rubes of all kinds from as far away as three hundred miles, and there were still the dance girls, and his hired thugs who saw that everything worked out to his advantage, whether that be in elections or the settling up of gambling debts.

The show was worth more than I owed, so when he bought me out, he gave me a choice of $20,000 cash in four payments or $30,000 in credit for lodging, meals, and gambling money at the casino. He knew me too well. I took the credit. I'd gone through that in the first year and a half. Now I owed him money. A couple weeks earlier he'd put limits on me—no more than four whiskeys a night; no more than twenty-five dollars gambling credit an evening.

"Mr. Coldwell? You all right?" the casino man said. He looked too spruced-up by half, his hair gummed down and shiny, his sleeve garters blinding fruity red.

"Sure I'm all right."

"Then you agree with me? I shouldn't ought to disturb Mr. Belden tonight?"

The other four were watching me, too.

They knew what the casino man was talking about.

In the morning, just down the block and around the corner, Marshal Shay was going to hang a twenty-one-year-old punk named Steve Belden. Jeremiah Belden's one and only son. Belden had let the jury find young Belden guilty, and let him subsequently be hanged, because there was a new circuit judge in the Territory, and he was one ruthless jurist, and a man who'd been trying to do damage to Belden for years. What better way than to execute Belden's son? I knew just what Belden was going through. I knew all about losing a son.

"You agree to just kind of drift on out of here so I won't have to call Mr. Belden?"

I saw another wink and another smirk get exchanged. I wanted to slap their faces, and let them know that I was a lot more than the simple soak I sometimes seemed to be.

But how could you convince people of that when they'd already turned you into somebody to snicker and whisper about?

"Mr. Belden, he's real upset about his kid," the casino man said. He leaned confidentially closer again. "Heard tell that he was up in his apartment this afternoon just cryin' his eyes out. Bawlin' like a baby." He frowned, shook his head. "So I sure wouldn't want to disturb him tonight with no problems of my own. No, sir, I sure wouldn't."

But I'd already spun away from the table, staggering a little, pointing myself toward the bat-wing doors, passing the dance floor where awkward farm girls in whorehouse dresses rubbed their tits up against fat men eager to have their egos deceived. There was noise and there was smoke and there was the high tart tang of raw cheap whiskey. It should have been fun as hell, all of it rolled up together that

way, but in the cold dark center of it there was just loneli-
ness and fear, and the silence of the grave. I pushed past the
Rochester lamps and the roulette wheels and the squirrel
cages and the long row of grinding slot machines.

Along the river that divided the town was a bench where
I sat most nights, trying to make some sense of my life, and
why it had taken its strange and terrible turn four years
earlier. And it was the river I always went to—after one
more brief stop.

2

My footsteps always fell where they wanted to, it seemed, taking me up a lane that wound around a huge oak tree and then switchbacked down a steep hill to where a graveyard lay in sober moonlight.

Some nights I knelt in the dewy grass so long, my trousers got wet. But I didn't mind, and scarcely noticed, because nothing mattered but the words I whispered. . . .

On the way to the graveyard, I came upon a pair of giggling lovers. The young man had his hand up the young woman's dress. The way they sat side by side against the back of the barn, you could tell they thought they had me fooled. But the way his shoulder moved told me what was really going on.

"It's that rummy," she whispered.

They giggled again.

As I got abreast of them, the young man, trying to impress his young lady, said, "You gonna say hello to us?"

"Hello," I said. I didn't look at them. I kept walking.

"Hey!" he shouted.

I just kept moving.

"Hey! You hear me, rummy?"

"Bill!" she whispered and slapped his arm.

I kept walking, the path winding up to the hill and the oak tree, and the dark fast creek below.

"Hey! I want you to apologize to my lady here for not greetin' her properly, not callin' her ma'am and showin' her proper deference."

I could hear him stand up in the vast silent night, creek of boot leather, jangle of change in pocket, and hear her whisper fiercely, "Leave him alone, Bill! He didn't hurt us any!"

But he was caught up in his own game now, and he no longer cared about impressing her. It was himself he wanted to impress.

I could smell her lilac water on him when he got within a foot or so of my back, and the high hard scent of his own sweat.

I stopped.

"Kid."

"You mean me, rummy?"

"I mean you."

I didn't turn around.

"Kid."

"Yeah, rummy?"

"I want you to walk back to your girl and leave me alone."

"And what happens if I don't, rummy?"

"Then I'm going to kick your fucking face in."

"You don't scare me, rummy."

She was a quick screamer, I'll say that for her, her shrill cry loud on the air even before I had turned fully around and planted the toe of my Texas boot in his crotch.

Shock showed on his face first. Then the pain. A lot of pain.

She was holding him even before he had fully sunk to the ground, teeth grinding, an ache in his throat and chest as he tried to pretend he could handle this amount of pain.

"I'm sorry," I said to her.

"You just git, you rummy. I don't know why they let you live in this town anyway."

"You could do a lot better for yourself than this guy, ma'am," I said.

But she was gone, lost in holding him infantlike to her fine full breasts, and cooing tiny half words, light as feathers, against the side of his pain-wracked face.

There was a cold clean smell to the moonlit creek as I knelt in front of the smallest of the tombstones and bowed my head and said those prayers you say when you don't quite believe that there really is a God and when you don't quite believe there isn't.

I said all the same old things, all those soft aching griefs I'd carried so long now, all those should haves and shouldn't haves that are the essence of remorse, all those little flickering memories that are like a nickelodeon that never runs down.

When I was done, I walked down along the creek and built myself a cigarette and stood there and listened to the rumble and thunder of the express as it came like an insane metal beast down the north-south tracks.

There was heat and light and rage in the way it assaulted the still prairie night, heat and light and rage I wanted to be part of, dragged away perhaps to some far city where I would magically become a different person. . . .

I stood so close, I almost got sucked under the wheels, into the steam and oil and grinding steel of its soul. . . .

And then it was gone.

And a vast stillness followed in its wake. And I stood so silent and alone I might have been standing suddenly on another planet—but then a crow cried, and I saw the moon behind the darkening clouds, and over the hill the two lovers I'd just passed were giggling again. . . .

It was time to see Evelyn.

3

Sometimes there was a sweet lark in the midnight trees, and sometimes, a quarter mile downriver, you could hear old black men sing sad river songs to themselves. There was a small encampment of blacks down there. They were welcome as cheap labor but not as residents, so they lived apart from the rest of Belden City.

Across the river and up in the wooded hills you could see, this time of night, the lights going out in the sweeping castlelike asylum called the Brooks House. In Belden City there were an awful lot of nervous jokes about the asylum, especially among children. They'd turned it into a mythic place of murderers and child stealers and monsters beyond description. The stories their parents told about the place weren't all that much different. Their monsters were just a little more adult was all.

I'd been here half an hour now. The September night was a bit chilly, but it was a sobering chilly. I built myself three cigarettes in a row and stretched my arms out on the back of the park bench where I sat. Naturally, I thought about myself and my life, how it had run and how it was probably going to keep on running. I tried to take two or three hours a day to feel sorry for myself. Self-pity's like anything else, if you want to get good at it, you have to practice.

There was a full moon that gave the river a glowing patina of gold. The last of summer's crickets sounded melancholy in the darkness.

Sitting there like that, I heard her coming. She passed this way most nights. It was one more reason for me to find my way to this park bench.

Her white uniform was brilliant in the gloom, her small cape dark on her slight shoulders. She came down the plank walk, past the empty park benches, past the small bandstand that came to raucous life every Fourth of July, and along the river that paralleled the bank where I sat.

She gave me a frail little wave when she saw me. I waved back.

Her name was Evelyn Saunders. She was a nurse at the hospital. She worked the three-to-eleven shift six nights a week. She was slight, pretty but not beautiful, dark-haired, and possessed of blue eyes that were vivid even in shadow.

Every once in a while she'd miss a night here, and I'd go back to my boardinghouse feeling empty and lonely and sorry as hell for myself. I'd come to depend on seeing her.

"This is between us, right?" she said when she sat down at a prim and proper distance from me on the bench.

"Right."

"I mean, you promise not to tell anybody?"

"We're back to this again, huh?" I smiled.

"You know how I get. If Dr. Snead ever found out what you and I do here . . ." Dr. Snead was her superior at the hospital. Nurses were expected to be models of probity.

"It's between us. I promise."

"Good." She grinned. "Then give me one."

"Yes, your highness."

'You're right. I was being rude. Please give me one."

"I like that better."

In a town like Belden City, among the folks who consider themselves respectable, an 1894 young lady does not partake of tobacco. Evelyn felt that if anybody ever found out, particularly anybody at the hospital, she would become the town's scarlet woman.

"Gosh, this tastes good," she said after I snapped a match on my thumbnail and put it to the smoke I'd built her.

She inhaled deeply. Exhaled. The smoke was a pearly blue against the round gold moon.

"I smelled winter today," she said.

"You smelled winter?"

"Sure. Don't you ever do that? Walk down the street on a nice fall day but all of a sudden there's this really cold breeze. And you can smell winter on it."

"Yeah, I guess I do, now that you mention it."

"I've smelled winter like that ever since I was a little girl."

Ordinarily, she didn't chatter on like this. Sometimes she was downright quiet, in fact.

But tonight she was talking fast and hard about nothing so she wouldn't have to talk about the one thing that was on both of our minds.

I said, "You going to see him?"

"I'm not sure."

"Maybe you should."

"Maybe it's not any of your business."

We were quiet for a time. I listened to the crickets. Watched bobbing fish create circles on the golden surface of river.

"I'm sorry I snapped at you that way."

"That's all right."

"No, it isn't. I really like you, Mitch. You're a good friend of mine." She stared at the moon, taking the last drags of her cigarette. "I'm glad I stopped here that night to see how you were."

That had been our first meeting. I'd been passed out on whiskey, sprawled across the park bench. Ever the dutiful nurse, she stopped to see how I was. She got me conscious and started talking to me about what whiskey can do to a man's body. Not to mention his soul.

"I'm glad you stopped, too," I said.

A brief silence.

"I don't know what to think anymore."

"I know you don't. It's pretty confusing," I said.

"Very confusing."

I shrugged. "You meant something to each other for a long time."

She sighed. "I guess you're right." She looked over at me. "Do you think Jeremiah will actually let them hang him?"

"Looks that way."

"That isn't like Jeremiah."

"No, but before he's a father, he's a businessman. And he knows that his son killed a man who was a part of this community. If Jeremiah stopped the hanging, the community would start to turn against him the way it never has before."

"So he lets Steve die?"

"He lets Steve die."

"His own son."

"His own son who shot a man in the back."

"Roy picked the fight, not Steve. If Roy hadn't been bothering me—" She put her hands in her lap. Stared down at them. "I bear at least some responsibility for all this, Mitch."

"And here I thought you were a sensible, intelligent girl."

"Well, it's true."

"It's not true. Not true a whit."

"Steve wouldn't have shot him if it hadn't been for me."

"I don't even want to talk about that, Evelyn. It's too crazy. I can understand why you feel sorry for Steve—but what happened had nothing to do with you. It had to do with Steve's temper. Nobody made him shoot Kedeher."

"You know, Jeremiah Belden blames me. Somebody said he wants to kill me."

"I heard that, too, but it's just town talk. You know how people are."

We sat there silent for a time. The breeze and the tobacco were dragging the drunkenness out of me.

"I don't suppose you tried it today," Evelyn said gently.

"No. Not today."

"You know what I told you. About the patient I had last year. How horrible his death was."

Ever since she'd met me, Evelyn had been trying to get me to quit drinking. She was afraid of what it would do to my health. She made me promise that sometime in the coming days I'd go one full twenty-four-hour period without a drop of alcohol. Just to see how it felt. Just to see if I could do it. So now, about once a week, she'd ask me if today had been the day.

"You think you'll ever really do it, Mitch?"

"Maybe I'm working up to it."

"Oh?"

"Last week I gave myself till eight o'clock every night to quit drinking for the day."

I wanted to tell her that maybe it would be easier if she agreed to marry me. That's what I was thinking, of course. I'd been schoolboy crazy about her since I met her. She made me feel alive again in ways I never thought possible. Not after what happened to me . . .

"You do seem a lot soberer lately."

"That's why. Because I'm cutting down."

"Maybe pretty soon you'll—"

But she stopped herself. Looked out at the river again.

I knew in moments like these that she'd never love me as I'd come to love her. I was twelve years older than she was. I had a fondness for the truth of the whiskey jug, and I had absolutely nothing to offer a woman who wanted a nice, settled life.

Plus, she had to deal with the hanging of a man she'd been engaged to. She'd broken it off about a month ago, but she obviously still cared for him a great deal. Maybe it was the nurse in her, always looking for people to help.

Steve Belden was Jeremiah's one and only boy. The mother had died early, so Jeremiah had raised the boy and he hadn't done a good job. On the one hand, he'd spoiled him pretty badly. Steve believed he could take anything he wanted. On the other hand, Jeremiah had never given the boy the least respect. Steve was handsome, some said pretty, and not especially proud of himself. When he drank, he could get to be a bully, good equally with fists and six-guns.

Roy Kedeher was a young cattleman who wanted to show the Beldens that he wasn't afraid of them, so he started following Evelyn around, pestering her to go out with him. One night he'd been pushing her especially hard when Steve showed up, drunk and angry. Steve tried to goad Kedeher into a fistfight, but Kedeher knew that young Steve would whip him. Kedeher walked away. He wouldn't turn around when Steve asked him to. Steve shot him three times in the back.

One of the shots entered just below Kedeher's right shoulder blade, traveling clean through his heart.

Nobody believed that Steve Belden was ever going to prison, let alone be executed. But they hadn't counted on Judge Raphael Kepplinger. He helped assemble the jury, and he helped give that jury enough courage to do what they needed to.

Tomorrow morning, Steve Belden was going to hang.

"I guess I'd better be going."

"It wasn't your fault, Evelyn. Not in any way."

"Maybe if I'd been firmer with Roy, I—"

"That's crazy talk and you know it."

She took a deep breath, exhaled, stared up at the moon.

"I'll bet that's what Steve's doing. Looking up at the moon the same way I am. In his cell, staring out through the bars. The moon always fascinated him. We'd go for buggy rides at night and he'd stop out on the old river road and just stand there and stare up at it for a long time."

Silence again.

"He's not all bad."

"Few men are, Evelyn."

"I mean, he can be very kind and very funny and very tender."

"Then you'll have some good memories."

"That's what my dad kept reminding me of whenever I'd say I wanted to break off with Steve. He'd remind me of how nice Steve could be when he wanted to."

I didn't say anything. One quick way to alienate people is to speak up against their parents. If Steve had raped and beaten her, her father would still have wanted her to go on seeing Steve. Her father was a poor man who had rich lazy dreams of easy wealth in the form of his pretty daughter marrying the richest young man in the Territory. And he didn't much give a damn how that rich young man treated his daughter, either.

She stood up, gathered her cape about her shoulders and said, "I wish I could just sleep for the next two days. I don't want to be awake when they hang him tomorrow."

I reached out my hand and she took it. "You'll be all

right, Evelyn. You're strong. You'll go on and find a new man and have a family for yourself and be happy."

She laughed sadly. "You sound like a swami."

I stood up. "That's about the only occupation I've never tried."

"I wish you knew how much pleasure you give folks with your shooting exhibitions, Mitch. Maybe you wouldn't make so much fun of yourself then."

She gazed up at the golden moon again. I thought of what she'd said, of Steve in his cell staring up through the bars at that very same moon, knowing he had only a few more hours to live.

She stood on tiptoe and gave me a quick kiss on the cheek, something she tended to do about once or twice a week.

"Good night, Mitch. You keep thinking about our twenty-four-hour plan, all right?"

"I'll do that."

Then she was gone, footsteps on the plank walk retreating, retreating.

4

On the way home I walked past the Wild West show and saw a light burning in the small cabin where supplies are stored.

Our stage Englishman, John Thomas Neville, who is actually from Delaware, was apparently still awake.

Not tired enough to sleep yet, I went up to the cabin door and knocked.

He wore a red-and-white-striped nightshirt and a cute little red-and-white-striped nightshirt hat that took some of the drama from the sawed-off shotgun he held.

"Oh, Mitch, it's you."

"Saw the light."

"Sure, sure, come in."

After he put the gun away and dragged a spindly rocking chair over for me to sit in, he went back to the armchair where he'd been reading and said, "You want some coffee?"

"No, thanks."

He smiled. "Good, because I didn't want to make any, anyway." Shook his white-maned head. "Was in a couple of saloons tonight listening to all the boys get worked up about the hanging tomorrow." He nodded to his book.

"Thought I'd let Mr. Poe try and help me forget all the things I heard tonight."

"Pretty bad?"

He glanced at the east wall. The others were covered with boxes of various supplies. But the east was a small gallery of posters and flyers depicting the grand and illustrious career of "John Thomas Neville, America's Favorite Englishman." By now, his mid-sixties, Neville had played in just about every carny and circus that plied these United States. And always the same role, too, the stuffy, top-hatted Brit that red-blooded Yanks found both fascinating and infuriating.

"I've been a lot of places, Mitch."

"You sure have."

"And I've seen a lot of hangings. Including one where a man's head got torn right off his shoulders."

"Kansas, wasn't it?"

"I already told you?"

"Uh-huh."

"Shit. And that's such a good story, too."

"No doubt about that."

"But I just don't have the stomach for it."

"For hangings?"

"Uh-huh. I'm all for capital punishment, that's the strange thing. There are things a man does—well, that he can't be forgiven for. Not on this earth, anyway. So in theory, I don't have any problem with him being hanged. But in practice . . ."

He sighed.

"You should've heard them tonight, Mitch. All drunked up and struttin' around and making bets on how many minutes it would take him to die and sayin' they wished they got to be the hangman."

"Steve Belden isn't exactly a sweetheart, John."

"Oh, I know that. In fact, as far as I'm concerned, he

should be put to death, but when you hear these young punks in the saloon—"

"I know what you're saying."

"It's pretty ugly, all that enthusiasm for watchin' another human being die. It should be a sad occasion, when you take somebody's life like that. You know, how it is when you have to put an animal down."

"Supposed to be more than a thousand people here tomorrow."

"Worst thing is, some of 'em will bring their kids."

I nodded.

"Why the hell would you want your little kid to see a hanging? I never could figure that out." Pause. "I ever tell you about the Indian that time?"

"Managed to piss on several of the white men when he was hanging up there?"

"I told you that already, huh?"

"Afraid so."

"Well, anyway, I always had a sneaking suspicion that they had it coming, those white men, I mean, havin' to be so all-powered close to the Indian so they could see his tongue go black and everything." He grinned. "So he pisses on them. That's pretty good in my book."

"Maybe Belden will piss on people tomorrow."

He shrugged. "I just worry about your friend Evelyn."

"Oh?"

"Sure. Everybody's talking about it."

"About what?"

"How old Jeremiah Belden blames her for everything that happened."

I snorted. "Hell, she didn't have anything to do with it."

"That's what a rational person would conclude, my friend, but remember, we're talking about Jeremiah Belden here."

For the first time I sensed some kind of trouble ahead. I

tried to dismiss it as just my usual midnight dreads, but I couldn't. Not quite. Something was going to happen, something bad, and I was sure of it.

"Well," I said, standing up.

"Mind if I say something?"

I had a pretty good idea of what it was going to be.

"You're sober."

"Pretty much."

"You're doing a hell of a lot better, Mitch."

"Thanks."

"Maybe someday you'll realize that you're a pretty decent man after all."

"Yeah," I said, "maybe someday I will."

I walked on home to the boardinghouse where I lived.

5

The shooting started somewhere around two that morning. By then I was in my bed at Mrs. Byrnes's boardinghouse, asleep in my small dusty room on the second floor.

The noise of gunfire woke me up, of course, but at first I didn't take it too seriously. Drunken gamblers who'd lost more than they could afford to lose occasionally staggered back to the casino in the middle of the night and fired shots in the air, demanding that Belden come downstairs and face them like a man. Belden, who was a businessman and not a fighter, usually did what I would have done, dispatched two of his prime bullies to quietly send the disgruntled gamblers on their way.

The gunfire was so loud, you could hear it clear the way up here, three blocks from where it was happening.

But after a few moments I realized that there were two, possibly three guns being fired, and that there were horses close by the gunplay, and that they were getting badly spooked.

Something serious was going on.

I threw my legs over the edge of the rumpled bed, reached for the pants and shirt I had hung on the bedpost, and grabbed my Colt Peacemaker and holster that I kept right on the floor next to the bed.

By the time I reached the street, I had a lot of company, other men and women running toward town to see what was happening.

The casino was quite—unusual for a Friday night—and as I passed it, following the crowd, I saw Jeremiah Belden stumble out. Like me, he looked as if he'd just awakened. Sleep lines crisscrossed his right cheek, his hair was mussed, and his eyes bore that glassy, distracted look of the half-asleep. His three-piece suit, tailor made for him in Denver, as were all his clothes, was rumpled and the front of it bore smudges of cigar ash. He had an outsize head and face, not unlike the busts you see of prominent Roman senators, and a stocky body just now starting to slide into middle age.

He looked at me with his usual mixture of scorn and pity. He had a brother, the story went, who was also a soak. It was said that this was the chief heartbreak of Belden's otherwise lucky life. He sent the brother five hundred dollars a month, the story went, to stay as far away from Belden City as possible.

He didn't say anything, just glared at me, and kept on going down the stairs.

I remembered what Evelyn had said earlier about smelling winter. It was on the air tonight, the grass shimmering with frost, the store windows showing thin veins of ice.

I wasn't asleep anymore, or drunk.

The slap-slap-slap sounds of running filled the dirt street. Beneath the full moon, in the middle of the night, half the town, it seemed, had turned out to see what had happened.

We started running, too, and had soon merged with the mob as it headed down to the end of the block and turned left, where a few people with flickering yellow torches could be seen.

As soon as we turned the corner, I could pretty much guess what had happened.

There had been a jailbreak, one that had gone awry in some way, and what we were about to see was the aftermath.

The jail was on the left, a two-story, red brick box with black bars on all the windows. The lower floor was the marshal's office. The upper floor held ten cells.

The four men with the torches had fanned out and were holding the rest of the crowd back from the three bodies lying in the center of the street.

I recognized the bodies right away—a night deputy, an auxiliary deputy, and Belden's son, Steve.

Everything seemed to stop momentarily as I looked over at Jeremiah Belden and saw his handsome face begin to disintegrate into confusion, disbelief, and pain. I knew what he was feeling because I'd gone through it myself just a few years back.

A deep animal sob filled his chest and then his throat and finally erupted from his mouth.

He pushed past me, he pushed past his hired bullies, he pushed past the white-haired old fart trying to look officious with his auxiliary badge shining in the torchlight.

He said nothing, looked at no one, simply went directly to the body of his son and knelt down next to him in the dusty street.

No matter what you thought of Jeremiah Belden otherwise, at this moment you couldn't help but feel what he was going through.

I'd never heard a group this big this hushed. The only sound was the ragged fluttering of the torch flame.

He must have knelt there two full minutes before he even so much as moved. He put a shaking hand out and touched the back of his son's head. And then he leaned down and kissed the boy tenderly on the cheek.

A few yards away a couple of women started sobbing.

After a time Belden stood up. One of his thugs stepped

forward to meet him and Belden said, "Get a wagon, Hank."

"Yessir." And departed.

Belden just stood there, then. He appeared to be so stunned that he wasn't quite sure what to do next.

From the front door, where he'd been standing with a Winchester cradled in his arms, came Marshal Walter Shay, a shambling, mumbling man whose shirtsleeves were always an inch too short and whose shirt often bore the stains of his most recent meal. But for all his middle-aged gawkiness, Shay was that most surprising thing of all in a gambling town, a reasonably honest man.

Everyone watched him now, everyone strained to hear.

What could he possibly say to a man as powerful as Jeremiah Belden about his son being killed?

"You want to come inside and have a cup of coffee?" Shay said.

At first there was no recognition in Belden's eyes. He hadn't seemed to hear Shay at all.

"Jeremiah," Shay said softly, even tenderly.

He put his hand on Belden's shoulder. Belden angrily brushed it away.

"You're going to regret this, Shay. I promise you that." Tears shook his voice.

"Do you want to hear what happened, Jeremiah? Do you want to hear the truth?"

Belden slapped him then, snake-quick, snake-deadly.

The slap rocked Walter Shay back on his heels.

"The truth is, Shay, my son is dead. The least you could've done was wait and hang him in the morning."

Shay rubbed his cheek. He looked pretty miserable just then, probably resenting being slapped in front of the citizenry this way, and probably feeling sorry for Belden, too. Shay had a son of his own.

"Steve broke jail, Jeremiah. Somebody slipped him a

key. And a .45. He got as far as the back door. These here
two deputies saw him. They followed him out the door.
Somebody had left a fresh horse for Steve at the side of the
jail. He got around to the front, and that's where they had
their shoot-out. I know your son's dead, Jeremiah, but so
are two of my men. And they've got families, too."

The wagon clattered up. The two thugs went about loading up Steve Belden's body, throwing a blanket over him so
gawkers couldn't get a good look-see.

After the body was set in the wagon bed, the wagon was
turned around and pointed north, out of town.

I was standing close enough to hear Shay say to Belden,
"I'm sorry, Jeremiah. I really am."

Belden didn't acknowledge Shay in any way. He turned
back toward the wagon.

Evelyn was standing nearby.

When he saw her, Belden glared at her, spat dramatically
in the dirt, got up on the wagon, took the reins, gave the
two horses some leather and started to pull out. Then he
looked down at Evelyn and said, "This is your fault, you
little bitch, and someday you're going to be sorry for it."

Folks didn't really start talking among themselves until
the wagon and its chinking noises had vanished around the
far corner. Women in shawls and scarves and mittens,
women in long calico dresses and mufflers, joined men in
sweaters and jackets and winter trousers in trying to find
words to express how sad they were for Jeremiah, who was
not so bad a man, all things considered, but how just it was
that Steve should be shot down this way, because he'd always believed himself to be above the law.

I went over to Evelyn, who was staring at the spot where
Steve Belden had been lying in the street.

I slid my arm around her and she leaned into the crook
of my arm. A few churchgoers who happened to notice us

looked displeased. I was a soak, and why would an otherwise decent young woman let me get this close to her?

"Why don't I walk you home?" I said.

She nodded and we set out.

The streets lamps cast all the storefronts into deep dark
shadow. Up this far, the crowd still around the corner, everything was quiet again, and you could hear an owl somewhere, and then a fast train in the distant mountain gloom,
and then, closer by, a child of no more than a few months
crying out for his mama in the night.

She was walking on her own now, no arm of mine
around her, and she was curiously silent.

"You all right?" I said.

"Did you see him?"

"Steve, you mean?"

"Yes. Why?"

"His face?"

"Yeah."

"How did he look?"

I shrugged. "The way dead men always look."

"Oh."

"Why?"

"I guess I was just curious is all. How he'd look at the
last, I mean. I guess I wonder that about myself, too. How
I'll look when the life's gone out of me." She walked a little more, quiet for a time. "Some people in the hospital,
right after they die they look very peaceful." She looked up
at me as we walked. "Do you ever think about how you'll
look, Mitch?"

"Guess not. Guess I don't much care how I look."

"We had a man in the hospital once. Doctor had to op-
erate on him. It was my first operation and the man was
scared so I got scared, too. He died in the middle of surgery
and he still looked scared. He was going to be buried that
way. With that scared look on his face. I just wondered—"

And then she broke.

I stopped and took her to me again.

She put her head against my chest and cried. Her tears were warm and wet on the flannel of my shirt. Her frail little body trembled.

"There are some things I should tell you, Mitch."

I smiled and kissed her forehead. "And I know what they are. How this was your fault somehow. And how you should have been nicer to Steve when he was alive. And how you wish you hadn't broken off with him. And—"

"No, Mitch, listen. What I wanted to say was—"

But there wasn't time.

Because that's when the naked man came running down the street, out of shadow and into the lighted part of town.

He was buck naked and he was shouting something about monsters being after him and he was coming right toward us.

"Oh, Lord," she said. "I'll bet he's from the Brooks House."

At first I'd had no explanation for myself as to who this man might be. Some drunk, I figured, chased out of his house by a wife fed up with his drinking.

But as soon as Evelyn spoke, I knew she was right.

No more than twenty yards behind him, their footsteps slapping the dirt street, came two men in business suits.

"Mr. Blackemore! You just slow down Mr. Blackemore! Everything will be all right! Nobody wants to hurt you!" the men called after him.

That was when he ran right into us, this Mr. Blackemore.

He was skinny, white-haired, probably sixty years old, and his dark gaze was hopelessly insane.

I grabbed him by one sinewy arm and held him for the men from the Brooks House.

"Much obliged," said the first of them, a burly, red-haired man with red whiskers and red muttonchop side-burns.

The two men in suits were so out of breath they were panting and sweating.

Mr. Blackemore looked as if he hadn't even been walking fast.

"We'll take you back now, Mr. Blackemore," said the second man. He was tall, slender, and had the professionally solemn air of an undertaker.

"But the monsters—" Mr. Blackemore said.

"There are no monsters, Mr. Blackemore," the undertaker said. "There really aren't."

"Thanks again," said the red-haired man.

"There are monsters," Mr. Blackemore assured me. He didn't have any teeth so he tended to spit when he spoke. He also had breath that could peel paint. "There really are."

"C'mon, now, Mr. Blackemore," both men said.

"They put me down in this room," Mr. Blackemore told me, "and there're monsters down there."

The two men looked at me and smiled.

Poor crazy bastard, their smiles said.

And I had no reason to doubt them.

"You should go with them, Mr. Blackemore," I said. "They'll help you."

"Will they keep the monsters from me?"

"Yes. And they'll give you a nice safe place to sleep, too."

He stuck his face in mine. "You promise."

"I promise."

"Maybe you're one of the monsters."

"Maybe I am, Mr. Blackemore. Maybe I am."

He looked at Evelyn. "You're really pretty, ma'am."

"Thank you," Evelyn said, and touched a tender hand to his elbow. "You go back with them now, Mr. Blackemore."

"You're real pretty."

Not until he was gone did I realize how badly Mr. Blackemore had smelled of sweat, urine, heat, and a slow dying.

They had turned him around and started guiding him back up the street the way they came.

That was also when I saw the bruises.

Mr. Blackemore looked as if someone had worked over his back and ribs with a board. The bruises were deep purple in the center, a sickly yellow color around the edges.

I saw this clearly because the two men took Mr. Blackemore beneath a street lamp.

"I wonder what happened to him," I said. "His bruises."

We started walking again.

"Maybe it's true," she said.

"Maybe what's true?"

"People who get put in there claim they're beaten sometimes. Maybe they beat Mr. Blackemore."

I was about to ask her more about the Brooks House when a familiar voice said, "You better get inside, Evelyn. He's nobody you want to be seen with."

We now stood in front of Evelyn's house.

"That's not very nice, Father," she said.

"It may not be nice, but it's true."

And with that her father got up from the front step where he'd been sitting, opened the door for her and said, "You'd better get in here now, Evelyn."

"Thanks for walking me home," she said.

"My pleasure."

She went inside.

Her father closed the door behind her, pausing just long enough to shoot me a dirty look.

6

The next morning being Saturday, I got to the Wild West show early, right after breakfast, so I could check everything out.

As you might expect, we had a lot of disappointed strangers on our hands, the town did, many of them having traveled all night to get here in time for the hanging.

But now there wasn't going to be any hanging, so the visitors had to figure out what to do with themselves.

The kids headed for the three general stores where they were likely to find the kinds of toys and books and soda pop that kids just naturally seem to love.

The women walked the boardwalk looking in store windows at bonnets, dresses, and hats; corsets, bustles, ribbons, and bows. It was pleasant to see a hard-scrubbed farm wife look ten years younger when her eyes lit on a frill that thrilled her. There was a sudden gentleness in her eyes then, as if she had forgotten for a time how to be female but now had suddenly remembered. A sea of bonnets, red and blue and yellow, bobbed along the boardwalks in the fine autumn sunlight.

The men, being men, tended to end up in liveries, blacksmith shops, feed stores, and, of course, saloons, where they'd promised their wives they'd be "only for a beer or two," but then started doing the kind of serious drinking that middle-aged men do to push back the grave momentarily and feel young again. It's not much different than their wives looking in dress shop windows.

A crowd stood for a couple hours before the scaffolding, looking up the stairs, smelling the fresh-sawn pine of the structure, pointing out where the rope and body would be hanging down right now if only things had gone according to schedule.

I had to hire some extras to help me with the show that day, young girls—girls being a hell of a lot more responsible than most boys their age—to help sell the lemonade and the popcorn and the red and black tangles of licorice so fresh it smelled like new rubber tires.

I had to get extra change, three big bags of it that could give even a weight lifter some back strain, and then check on one of the horses and make sure his diarrhea had cleared up. A horse like that can spoil the show for a crowd of eager kids.

The hard September sunlight showed that most of the exhibits in The Belden Family Wild West Spectacular were in need of a coat of paint and at least some minor carpentry.

The Indian Wars exhibit—lots of stock photographs of Indians and U.S. Cavalry and artifacts such as tomahawks and spears and a few knives—needed its canvas depiction of Chief Blackhawk touched up; the Hanging Tree Exhibit—photographs of outlaws swinging from ropes; plus pistols, gun belts, hats filled with bullet holes, hangman's nooses, and a couple of gleaming six-pointed badges that allegedly belonged to Pat Garrett and Wild Bill Hickock respectively—needed some replacements in its wooden flooring; and the Most Dangerous Animals—stuffed rattlesnakes, bobcats, gila monsters, and alligators—was in bad need of a serious dusting and cleaning. In the sunlight, a fine patina of silver dust covered everything.

Part of the time, when I'd gathered a group around me, I told tales, most of them of the tall variety, about Wild Bill and Wyatt Earp and Ben Thompson and the James Boys, all of those men who beat death by getting themselves buried as legends. The crowd didn't want to know about the drinking or the whoring that gave at least two of them cases of syphilis they never did get rid of and probably passed on to their wives, or all the crooked cowtown dollars they took, or the way they sometimes killed in cold blood; no, that kind of tale would damage the legend. And it was my duty, as the high priest of horseshit, to keep that legend alive.

This was the Wild West show, an embarrassment to anybody who'd ever been to Billy Cody's extravaganza, but enough to keep the local children enthusiastic as long as the rides were in good running shape. Jeremiah Belden had brought in a small carousel and a merry-go-round.

Throw some calliope music over all this, put a "bally" out front doing his job—"The Wild West at its most terrifying! See the bullet that killed Jesse James! See the gun belt worn by Billy the Kid! See the rifle used by Buffalo Bill"—and you've got a show that's no better or worse than a hundred other ones out here in the territories.

By ten o'clock I had everything open and set up and ready.

It was about then that John Thomas Neville showed up in his dark Edwardian suit, his black top hat, his frilly white shirt, and his dark string tie. With his windblown white hair, his fierce blue eyes, and hatchet nose, he was mighty impressive-looking, especially when you're ten years old and eager to be impressed.

"We're going to have one hell of a day," he said, striding up as he tapped his top hat in place.

"Sure looks like it."

"Some of these pretty girls make me dizzy. I thought I was past all that kind of stuff."

"Not when she looks like that," I said, nodding to a young blonde in a blue bonnet and bustle.

He looked toward town. "You see 'em around the scaffolding?"

"Yeah."

"Like little kids disappointed that the Easter Bunny didn't show up."

"They came all this way for a show."

"Some show. Watchin' a man kick and wiggle and shit his pants. And then die."

"Well, at least they got their way on the last thing. He sure died."

"I hear there was a lot of gunplay."

I nodded. "A real lot."

"I also hear that old Jeremiah sat up in his casino most of the night drinking and making threats about Evelyn."

"Heard that myself."

"You think it'll come to anything?"

"I sure as hell hope not."

"Well, guess we'd better get to it."

I went into the train caboose we used as an office. The walls were covered with circus posters from the days when I was a star attraction often spoken of as the equal of Annie Oakley. Several posters showed me in fancy cowboy duds standing on horseback while shooting birds from the sky. The duds I actually wore; the horseback thing was total fantasy. For one thing, even though I grew up on a farm, I've always been a bit leery of horses, my younger brother having been kicked nearly to death by one, and for another, I've never used a rifle in my act. Always a six-shooter.

I walked past the cracked leather couch where I sometimes napped on slow business days, the wooden filing cabinet where I kept our cash records and a pint bottle of sipping mash, and the desk where I kept the one and only photograph I had of my wife and son. My cousin in Nebraska was a photographer, one of those men who can always be seen lugging around his bulky camera and heavy glass photographic plates. He'd outdone himself that soft May Sunday of long ago. Heather had never looked more beautiful, nor our seven-year-old son Mac more handsome. Even I didn't look so bad in an angular, worried way. That was how I always photographed, looking worried as hell.

The office smelled of dust, sunlight, and cigar smoke.

From the bottom right drawer of the desk I took out a sack of candy and handed it to Neville.

"Can I trust you this time?"

"It's a curse, my sweet tooth."

"You know how Belden's been on my ass about expenses, Neville. He wants me to be able to justify every penny."

"I know." He tried to look hangdog. Actually, he couldn't wait to get his fat pink hands on this sack of peppermints.

"He counts up the ticket stubs and sees that we had only eighty-six paid admissions, which should mean no more than one bag of this candy—but we're going through two, three bags a Saturday."

He found his dignity again, pulled himself up, bedecked himself in the splendor that properly belonged to Shakespearean thespians and said, "You can put your trust in me, Mitch. I swear that on the great bard's grave."

The great bard's grave.

"Sure," I said, and reluctantly handed him the bag of peppermints.

The trick they still liked best of all was shooting backward over my shoulder and knocking down four tin cans set along the top of a fence.

They enjoyed watching me shoot ten out of ten dinner plates tossed into the air; they applauded when I put a bullet dead through the center of an Ace of Spades playing card held twenty feet from me; and they cheered when I shot out the flames atop several tiny candles.

But they still liked the backward shooting best. To the young mind, it was probably the most baffling.

I did three shows that day. The crowd at the last one was the kind I liked. There was a lot of *oohing* and *aahing* and poking each other in the bony ribs with bony elbows.

I worked inside a corral out in back of the show. Kids were two deep, lining up around the front half of the show, leaving me clear to use the back half for my shooting.

The kids talked a lot about the hanging, and how disappointed they were. But there was a breathless quality to how they talked about the jailbreak and the shoot-out and the three dead men. I could tell that this would soon enter that mythic realm where youngsters liked to live. They would embellish the story each time they told it, making it a little more engrossing each time out, until even they would soon be unable to tell the difference between reality and myth. Myth was always a hell of a lot more fun.

Around three the sunlight started to fade, and the long purple shadows brought with them a real autumn bite.

The exhibits had started emptying out about the time I was finishing up my last show.

I walked up and watched the kids on the rides for a while and then went over and told the calliope player that he could knock off early if he helped me throw the tarps over the exhibits. He gladly agreed. He was a colored man who had finally been accepted by the colored folks who lived nearby upriver. He had a girl now and she'd come to obsess him the way only a girl can obsess a man.

My Shakespearean friend was drunk. Most folks couldn't tell, but I could. His words weren't quite so clear now; and every fifth or sixth line there was a tiny hesitation, hootch making him uncertain of what words came next.

Farm women in gingham and calico, farm men in heavy coats and flat black hats, came by to gather up their children. Their wagons would be piled high with groceries and merchandise from the general store. Tonight there would be store treats for the entire family after a heavy meal and maybe a hymn or two led by Mother.

I was just telling Neville to close up when I saw Sonia Eckstrom, a formidable blonde woman in nurse-white dress and nurse-blue cape, walk over to me. She was a Swedish immigrant, having arrived twelve years ago with her widowed father. She was the head nurse at the hospital.

"I am looking for Evelyn," she said when she reached me.

She pronounced it "lewking." Her tone was cold, not even feigning politeness. She knew that Evelyn and I were friends of a sort, and disapproved. Like Evelyn's father, Sonia believed that Evelyn should have put up with Steve Belden's shortcomings and married him anyway.

I pulled my railroad watch from my trouser pocket. "It's four o'clock. She isn't at the hospital?"

"No. And on Saturdays she is supposed to start at twelve, three hours earlier."

"I haven't seen her. Have you talked to her father?"

She nodded. The fading light softened her, giving her plain face a real prettiness. It was as if she didn't want me to see this soft side.

"I don't know about him."

"I'm not sure what you mean."

"Do you know him?"

"A little bit, I suppose." I smiled. "He isn't exactly ever happy to see me."

She didn't smile at all. She wasn't exactly ever happy to see me, either.

"He said that she got up this morning and made him

breakfast and went shopping and then came back and got ready for work."

"What's wrong with that?"

She shook her blonde head. "I walked up and down the streets for the last half hour asking any of the merchants if they'd seen her this morning. None of them had."

"Maybe you asked the wrong merchants."

She shook her head again. "I've worked with Evelyn for two years now. I know exactly where she shops. Anyway, the main street is not so big. Somebody should have seen her."

"Are you saying that her father lied?"

"I'm saying that I don't know what I'm saying. He—acts funny. That's all I know to say."

"You mean as if he's hiding something?"

She nodded. "Yes. That's the right way to say it."

At first I'd thought she was maybe overplaying all this. There could be a logical reason for her disappearance. For one thing, Evelyn had obviously been very upset about Steve being killed last night.

"Maybe she just wanted to be alone somewhere," I said. "After last night, I mean."

"Maybe."

I saw the colored man standing in the center of the empty midway, waiting for me to help him finish closing up. The Most Dangerous Animals exhibit took two pairs of hands to close off, even though both of the bobcats were so old their teeth were starting to fall out. Fortunately, they could still sound pretty frightening.

"Well, if I see her, I'll certainly tell her that you are looking for her."

"I would appreciate it," she said.

She glanced around once more at the shambles of my little show. Tart disapproval sparkled in her blue eyes. She shook her head almost imperceptibly—at both me and my show, I assumed—and then walked away without saying good-bye. I had to admire the way she walked, purposeful yet definitely female. She was a strong woman and there wasn't anything wrong with that at all.

I went and helped the colored man get out of there as soon as possible. Unlike me, he had a life outside the Wild West show.

7

In case you're wondering, yes, I am the fellow who shot his own twelve-year-old son to death.

I'm sure you read about it. The territorial papers wrote it up for six months running, how a sharpshooter had used his son as part of the act and then accidentally killed him. Mac had always wanted to put the cigarette in his mouth, turn to me in profile, and have me shoot the cigarette in half from several feet away. He thought it would be a lot of fun. I wasn't worried about it. I switched from regular load bullets to what we call gallery loads, which run just forty-one grains and use a much lighter load of black powder.

My wife was there that warm South Dakota dusk at the fairgrounds when Mac moved his head—we'd practiced for two weeks and he hadn't moved his head once—and the bullet got him above the ear. Later, after I just kept repeating over and over that I'd used a gallery load, the doc had just looked and me and said, "Mr. Coldwell, it's just one of those freak accidents. It shouldn't have killed him, but it did."

Only two things I can much recall. The frozen moment when Mac was hit and then stopped moving completely before sinking to the ground; and Heather's cries. She'd miscarried one night a few years earlier and had cried the same way—the cry of horror and loss and rage that doesn't know where to light.

There was a funeral, and there were stern editorials calling for keeping people out of sharpshooting exhibitions, and there were a dozen nights when I went up to our bedroom to sleep, only to be turned away.

Heather never blamed me, or at least she claimed she didn't, but I never slept with her again after Mac's death. In fact, the only time I can remember holding her for any length of time was after the funeral, when we stood in the ridiculously sunny morning and looked at the raw hole in the earth that would forever be our only child's home. Then she held me, held me so tight she scared me, and cried so hard I was wondering if she might not have gone quietly insane.

Thirty-four days after the funeral, I came home from the hardware store to find a wagon loaded with several familiar-looking trunks standing in front of our house. The wagon belonged to an old colored man who did odd jobs for people around town.

Heather came out, turning to lock the front door behind her. She hadn't seen me as yet. When she did, she didn't look either surprised or saddened.

She came over to me, took my hand, and said, "I'm going back to Ohio, Mitch. I've thought about it and it's the best for both of us. I know how much you loved Mac and how sad you are but I just won't ever be able to get around it. I'll be sending you divorce papers."

I knew better than to say anything. She was one of those women who made her mind up only after long, purposeful deliberation. Once it had been made up, there was no changing it. Ever.

The first few days, all I did was sit in the front room and build myself cigarettes and drink some home brew we'd made in the spring. A couple of times I cried so hard I threw up—missing Mac and Heather and the man I used to be, I suppose—and one time I put my fist into the wall so hard, I broke a few knuckles.

At midnight of the second day, I went to the full-moon graveyard and knelt in the dewy grass where the new headstone had been set deep into the earth. I held the stone tenderly, as if it were Mac himself in my arms, and this time my tears were gentle ones, tears of pure grief. I told him how much I loved him and how sorry I was that the trick had gone wrong and how I would see him again someday. Heather had always been the religious one, but that night in the graveyard, I felt giddy with the prospect that I would in fact see my son again someday.

Afterward, I went home and slept for thirty-six hours. I woke up, shaved, bathed, put on fresh clothes, and then walked downtown to consult a land dealer. He sold our home in less than a full working day. Twenty-four hours after that, I was on a train headed west. That summer there were a number of Wild West shows crisscrossing the plains. One of them was sure to hire me.

The serious drinking started on the train that night. I'd never been one for whiskey, but that night I learned of its mercies and blessings—total oblivion. I woke up in the middle of Colorado with three old women glaring at me. I'd gotten argumentative in the bar car so they stashed me in a coach car where my snoring woke up the old ladies.

That was three years ago, during which time I'd worked for a couple of shows and then started my own. My pride was that my drinking had never interfered with my duties, which was true. But it interfered with everything else. By the time I reached Belden a year and a half ago, I was in especially sorry shape, and so I lost my show by gambling, and ended up an employee of Jeremiah Belden.

* * *

I was nearing my limit of whiskey and gambling credit when I realized that I was out of tobacco. Belden keeps several brands up near the slot machines. He charged three times the going rate, but this time of night, who was going to complain?

Saturday night there was a big crowd, including a railroad section crew working a few miles to the east. No crowd except maybe cowpunchers is rougher than section crews. After a certain number of drinks, they invariably turn mean. Belden knew enough to prepare for any trouble. Six men with Winchesters were positioned around the casino and dance floor and bar. They were the type of men who would shoot you in cold blood if Belden gave the order.

I was just telling the girl at the tobacco stand my brand when I looked up and saw Bob Saunders, Evelyn's father. He was alone. He went straight from the bat-wing doors to the bar, ordered a whiskey and stood there sipping it.

I decided to visit him.

"Mr. Saunders?"

One thing about being a soak, you quickly learn how to be a supplicant. How to grovel before people who despise you, so maybe they'll despise you just a little bit less. But of course, if anything, they despise you just a little bit more. I'd had enough blackouts in this town that I wasn't sure who I'd insulted, or vomited in front of, or made some kind of scene with. I was that kind of drunk.

He had his sneer ready when he turned around. "I didn't invite you over for a drink, Coldwell."

"I know that. And I'm not inviting myself, either. I just wondered if you'd heard from Evelyn."

"How'd you know about that?" He wore a celluloid collar that had been washed enough to be worn thin on the edges, and a white dress shirt yellowed slightly from going too long unworn. Evelyn had told me that her father belonged to a particularly uncharitable Christian sect that did not believe in alcohol, sex except for procreation, or fancy duds.

I wondered why he was wearing his version of fancy duds tonight.

"Sonia Eckstrom stopped by my show and asked if I'd seen her. Said she was late to work. She seemed worried."

He looked down at his whiskey then back up at me. Before he spoke, he gunned his drink in a gulp, turned and ordered another one, and then turned back to me while the bartender fixed him up.

"You don't have any business askin' about my daughter."

He was a rabbity little man with a large brown wart on his small plugged nose and a cracker meanness in his pale blue eyes. Easy to imagine him caught up in the fanatical hatreds of fundamentalism.

The bartender brought his drink, interrupting us.

He sipped and said, "I'm gonna tell you somethin' even though it ain't your business."

I just waited.

"She decided to leave town for a while. You know, with what happened and all last night. She cared for Steve Belden a lot more'n most people knew."

That might be true enough, I thought, but why would she leave town?

"Where did she go?"

"Up by the territorial line. Got some kin up there. She'll be with them for a while."

"Kind of funny, her leaving without letting the hospital know."

"She said I should let them know," he said.

"Well, if you did, Sonia Eckstrom didn't get the message until real late in the day."

"I don't work for Sonia Eckstrom."

He wasn't telling me the truth. I'd had too much to

drink, and I didn't know him well at all, but his story just didn't make any sense.

Evelyn was one of the most dutiful, responsible people I'd ever known. She'd never leave town without telling the hospital first. She was the kind of person who would probably even get her own replacement before leaving.

"How'd she get there?"

"What?"

"How'd she get there?" I said.

"Train, how else would she get there?"

"Train in the middle of the night?"

"Early morning train. Six A.M."

"She was on that one?"

He nodded. "She sure was."

"Was Leifer the conductor?"

He shrugged. "S'pose so. That time of morning and all. That'd be his run."

I stared at him for a time. "She's your daughter."

"What's that supposed to mean?"

"It means I don't think you're telling me the truth. And that makes me suspicious, why you'd lie about her."

"Well, I can say one thing, anyway, Coldwell."

"What's that?"

"Least I never shot my own son."

I felt my cheeks burn and anger quicken my pulse and my right hand form into a fist. But what was the use? People hit you with what was handy. And with me, that would always be the handiest weapon of all, how I'd killed Mac that night.

"Believe it or not, Saunders, I care about your daughter."

"So do I."

"That why you wanted her to marry Steve Belden even though he wouldn't settle down?"

"I've had a belly full of you, you know that, Coldwell?"

With that he turned his back to me, pounded on the bar for another drink.

I drifted back past the line of slots and the faro tables and the roulette wheels and the squirrel cages and the poker tables to the dance floor.

I got two tickets from the cashier and then went and found me the dance girl who most resembled my former wife Heather so that when I closed my eyes and we danced slow to the sweet fiddle music, I believed for a few seconds that it actually was Heather, and that none of it had happened, that Mac was playing in the long grass with his collie Scout, and that she and I were still the best of friends and the best of lovers.

"Aw, shit, Mitch," Lulu said.

"Huh?" I said, opening my eyes.

"Yer doin' it again."

"Doing what?"

But I already knew what she was going to say.

"Yer cryin' again. Those goddamn tears runnin' down yer cheeks. It's embarrassin'. That's why I hate dancin' with you."

And with that lovely Lulu left, picking herself a bow-legged miner for a paid-for partner.

The tears meant that I was starting to get seriously drunk. I decided to walk over to the park where I usually met Evelyn.

I was just headed out the front doors when I looked over and saw that Bob Saunders had himself a new drinking partner, Jeremiah Belden.

Belden was the kind of man Christians were always denouncing.

What had brought he and Bob Saunders together, anyway?

8

I spent the next hour walking along the river. Over the past six weeks, I'd been playing with Evelyn's advice to try weaning my way off alcohol. I gave myself a few hours in the evening to imbibe, and I was stopped before I felt falling-down drunk. I'd been pretty bad on occasion, falling face first to the floor, throwing up before I reached the back alley, even peeing my pants while I slumped unconscious at the bar.

Pretty good reasons, I suppose, for people to smirk and snicker whenever they saw me. Even better reasons to stay away from me. I'd been adjudged to be less than human, and that's how I would forever stay in this town's eye.

I walked off the drunk I'd been building.

I followed the railroad tracks, shining sleek silver in the moonlight, along the bend in the river and up into the foothills where the autumn trees were fiery even at night.

Hoarfrost was starting to cover everything. I could see my breath. My knuckles were hard from the cold, just as my nose and cheeks were numb. But by God, I was sober, real sober, by the time I returned to town.

I went straight to the marshal's office. Shay could usually be found there till ten every night. He was a widower, and his only son had moved to Omaha to study law, and ever since he had the curse of a lonely man about him.

When I reached the plank walk, I looked between the curtains of the barred front window and there he was at his desk, filling in a long leatherbound ledger with a pen he kept dipping into a small bottle of black ink. His light came from a fancy flowered vase lamp, one that most men would think too female to use. But Shay didn't give a damn about things like that. He openly mourned his wife's passing, and his office was filled with sentimental reminders of her.

There was a bell above the front door. It jangled merrily as I came inside.

Shay looked up, all skin and bone and white hair now that he'd reached fifty, Ichabod Crane with a badge as some wag had remarked. And there was that gaunt New England look to him, one that his western clothes and double six-guns couldn't quite take away.

He wore a western vest with a six-pointed star on the right side, a faded yellow corduroy shirt about an inch too short in the sleeves, and a pair of red flannel longjohns that made a red swatch at the top of his shirt.

"Evening, Marshal."

He nodded, looking at me closely. He played the game every adult citizen of this town always played with me after sundown. Is he or isn't he? Drunk, that is.

He gave a little start of surprise when he realized that I was sober.

"I was about to have some coffee, Coldwell. Care for some?"

"Appreciate it."

He came up from behind the desk in segments until he'd reached his full six-two. Then he snatched up a couple of metal cups from the edge of his desk and went over to a potbellied stove where a coffeepot stood. There was a heavy blue cloth next to it. The pot handle would be very hot.

One wall of the office was two rows of rifles and shot-guns and Wanted posters. Another wall was framed photographs of presidents and territorial governors and other prominent people who had passed this way. The third was a library. Deputies generally didn't have much schooling. Shay believed that they had to have at least a minimal education to do their job properly, to be a truly modern deputy, so he was schoolmarming them himself in the basics of English, mathematics, history, and geography. His wife had been a teacher. I suspected this was one more way he had of honoring her.

He set my coffee down on the arm of my wooden chair then went back behind his desk and sat down.

"You've had a pretty exciting twenty-four hours," I said, making conversation.

"Not the kind of excitement I want, believe me. I have a son, too. I know what Jeremiah is going through."

"You don't think he was the one who slipped Steve the key and the gun?"

He had brought his coffee to his lips and had been blowing on it. Now he stopped. "You came over here for a reason, Coldwell. What was it?"

I shrugged. "Just to get your sense of what happened last night. How you explained how a prisoner got hold of a key and a gun."

"The city council appoint you to question me, did they?"

"I don't have the right to ask as a citizen?"

"I guess I never quite thought of you as a citizen, Coldwell. Most citizens don't crawl around on bar floors on their hands and knees."

I dropped my eyes. That kind of thing hurt to hear. Everybody has a certain way he sees himself or herself.

Crawling around on bar floors, as I had done, didn't exactly jibe with my sense of myself as a quiet, dignified man.

"I'm sorry."

I looked up.

"I said I'm sorry, Coldwell. I shouldn't have said that. Not my place to judge you. God knows, you had a tragedy that most of us wouldn't be able to handle at all."

He sipped coffee.

"But it does kind of piss me off that you'd come over here nosing around this way."

"I don't have the right to nose around?"

He nodded his white head. "Sure you do. I just wish I knew why you were doing it. Everybody in this town seems to think that I gave Steve that key and that gun. But I didn't. I was just as surprised as everybody else."

"That isn't why I'm here, about Steve I mean. I'm here about Evelyn."

"Evelyn Saunders you mean?"

"Yes."

"What about her?"

"She's disappeared."

"Oh, hell, now I know what you're talking about. Sonia Eckstrom was over here this afternoon all het up."

"You looked into it?"

"She left a note that she wanted to get away for a while."

"You saw the note?"

"No, but her father said she left one. Why wouldn't I believe him?"

"He tell you she left on the early train?"

"Yep."

"Went up the Territory to visit some kin?"

"That's what he told me."

I said, "You talk to Karl Leifer, the conductor?"

"About what?"

"About putting her on the train?"

"No. Why would I talk to Leifer?"

"Well, I asked her father if anybody saw her get on the train and he said Karl Leifer did."

"You're saying what exactly about her father?"

"I don't know."

"Sounds to me as if you're calling him a liar."

I shrugged. "I just think it's funny."

"That she left?"

"Right."

He sat back, stared at the festive flowered lamp on his desk. He looked at it fondly.

He turned back to me. "I'm told you sat in the park with Evelyn sometimes."

"Guess so."

"Then you probably got to know her at least a little."

"Yes, I did."

"Then you know the long, sad tale of her engagement to Steve Belden. She loved him but she just couldn't tolerate the way he acted sometimes. Between you and me, Steve got all the worst traits of Jeremiah, and none of the good ones."

"I've heard that before."

"Anyway, here's a young woman in love with this young man, but she feels forced to call off the wedding. Right?"

"Right."

"But that doesn't mean her feelings for him stopped."

"I don't suppose it does."

"Then he gets himself shot trying to break jail— Well, just imagine yourself this young woman. With all these complicated feelings. With the eyes of the whole town on you. Wouldn't you be tempted to get on a train and leave town?"

"I see what you're saying. But she's not the kind of young woman who'd go off without notifying somebody."

"She did notify somebody. Her father."

"But besides her father, I mean. She's a very responsible woman."

"I know that."

"So it seems to me she'd at least get ahold of somebody at the hospital."

"At that time of morning?"

"Well," I said, "leave them a letter if nothing else."

"But you're forgetting something, Coldwell."

"What's that?"

"Her state of mind. Think about that for a while."

"I walked her home after the shooting. She was upset, but she wasn't hysterical or anything."

"But what about when she gets inside and lies down in the dark and it all starts rushing in on her? She had to have some real complicated feelings about everything."

I sighed. I wasn't going to convince him. He wasn't going to convince me. "Then you don't think anything happened to her?"

"Such as what?"

I smiled. "You know, that's funny."

"What is?"

"I've been worrying about her all day, but I guess I've never really thought about what might have happened to her."

"In all likelihood, what happened to her was that she got on a train early this morning and went to visit some kin up the Territory."

"I guess you could be right."

"And in all likelihood, what will happen to her next is that she'll get homesick for her house and her job at the hospital and she'll come back in a few days."

"You make it sound pretty simple."

"That's one thing I've learned in this business."

"What is?"

"That people keep trying to complicate things. But that

most things are pretty simple. Take most so-called 'disappearances.' About ninety percent of them are just some little boy or some fed-up adult wandering off for a few hours to get his bearings back. But if I said that to every scared mother or worried father who came in here, they'd run me out of town. My explanation'd be too simple for them. They want it all gussied up and complicated."

I stood up. "You could be right."

"I am right."

He stood up, too. Put forth his hand. We shook.

"Sorry about that crack I made, about your drinking."

"It's all right."

"No, it isn't. My wife always said I had a petty streak, and she was right. I try to keep it in check, but I don't always manage."

I pointed to the cup. "You make good coffee."

"Actually, my deputy made that. I like mine a little stronger."

I went to the door. Put my hand on the knob.

"So you don't think there's anything to worry about?"

"Not a damn thing, Coldwell. I really don't."

"I appreciate your time."

"Now don't go bothering people about this, because I'll be the first one to hear about it and I'll just have to climb on your back, then, and neither of us want that now, do we?"

"No," I said. "No, I guess we don't."

I left.

9

The casino and the saloons were still noisy on Front Street, lewd in the otherwise quiet prairie night. I thought of stopping in for a beer, then decided no. I was able to limit myself to three hours of drinking a night. No sense in falling back. At least in three hours I couldn't get drunk enough to crawl around on the floor or soil my trousers.

When I reached Badger Street, I started to turn left, toward the boardinghouse where I slept, but then found myself following my feet to the right.

Karl Leifer, the conductor who'd allegedly put Evelyn on the train this morning, lived two blocks away in that direction. He worked the short run for the Rock Island line and so managed to be home most nights.

Walking alongside small white houses that looked snug and safe in the moonlight, I thought of my wife and son, and how we'd always had dreams of the same kind of life.

When she'd left me, I'd hated her, of course. Not much else I could feel but hatred. But now, a few years later, relatively sober and able to see things more clearly, I didn't blame her.

We'd come to a long, sad end, and there had been nothing for her to do except walk away. The divorce papers had come almost at once. By now she could be settled down and starting another family. I hoped she was.

Leifer's street was filled with the gopher holes left behind by crews putting in telephone lines. Pretty soon half the folks in Belden City would have telephones. About forty percent had them now.

Loose shoveled dirt covered the lawns. The holes had been dug but the poles hadn't been set in, and the cleaning up was a few days away yet.

When I reached the Leifer house, which was really more of a cottage surrounded by a picket fence, I saw no lights. Reasonable people, decent people, were asleep at this hour.

I moved several yards down the sidewalk. A dim light shone in the back window. I assumed it was the kitchen.

I decided to walk back there and find out for myself.

The grass soaked my boots. Next door, a dog started some sharp relentless barking. He got louder as I got closer.

I reached Karl Leifer's back window and peered inside. In the dirty yellow glow of a kerosene lamp, a stout bald man smoked a pipe and poured himself yeasty golden beer from a small bucket.

He must have been used to hearing the neighborhood dogs because the barking didn't seem to interest him at all.

I raised my hand to knock on the small back door, but just as I put knuckles to wood, I heard a carbine cock behind me and felt the cold steel muzzle of a gun barrel touch the back of my head.

"What the hell're you doin' back here?"

"Came to see Karl."

"Bullshit." It was a female voice, and an angry one. "Karl don't have no callers this time of night. He's got to be up at four A.M."

"You want to ask Karl?"

"Good thing my dog woke me. Since the mister died, he's the only protection I got."

She hadn't seemed to hear me. "Knock on the door," I said. "Tell Karl that Mitch Coldwell wants to see him."

"Coldwell? You run that trick show?"

"Yep."

"Took my niece to that. Didn't think it was worth a damn."

Not only was she threatening me with a gun, she was giving my show a bad review.

"Lemme have that .45 of yours. You hand it back here nice and easy."

I took it out and handed it back nice and easy.

"Knock on the door."

"What?" I said.

"Knock on the door."

By this time I was getting curious about Karl Leifer. A dog was barking, two people were talking, and now I was knocking on the door and he didn't so much as look up.

"Knock louder."

I knocked so loud the door hinges started to rattle.

"One more time."

"What's wrong with him?"

"Thought you knew him, mister."

"I didn't say I knew him. I said I came to talk to him."

"Hearin's bad. In the war, he fought for the Rebs. Stood too close to a cannon too many times or somethin' like that."

Inside, Karl Leifer turned abruptly around and looked at the door. The funny thing was, this time I hadn't knocked. Karl must have received a spirit message.

He got up from the high stool where he'd been sitting at a table and walked back to the door. He wore a blue flannel nightshirt and some kind of slippers that slapped as he walked.

He got the door open and said, "Yes."

"Karl. Caught this man peekin' in your window."

He angled his head to the side, squinted as he listened. Karl seemed to receive sound a few seconds later than everybody else.

"Oh, hello, Maude. You're up kind of late."

"Not up late, Karl. Woke up late. By this man."

"Oh."

Karl looked me over. It took him a while to figure out who I was. Then, "You're that carnival fellow."

"Mitch Coldwell."

"Right. Mitch Coldwell. What can I do for you?"

"I just wanted to talk to you a little bit."

"If he wanted to talk to you, why didn't he knock on the front door?" Maude said. I still hadn't gotten a glimpse of her.

"That's a fair question, son," Karl Leifer said mildly. His small house smelled good, of sweet smoking tobacco and fresh beer and warmth from a stove.

"I was just walking around to the back because I saw a light on."

"Guess I'm not sure why you'd want to talk to me, anyway," Karl said.

"Well, if you'd invite me in, I'd tell you."

He looked at me and looked at Maude and said, "I guess it's all right, Maude. I appreciate you looking out for me."

She came into view finally. She was in a nightshirt, too, maybe sixty-five years old, maybe eighty pounds dripping wet right after she ate two pounds of butter, and carrying a Winchester that was absolutely the latest model. And she wore a black patch over her right eye. Somehow her looking like a pirate didn't surprise me any.

"You sure you'll be all right, Karl?"

"I'll be fine, Maude. Thanks again."

"You think I could have my gun back?" I said.

She glanced at Karl.

He nodded.

With a little clucking sound, she handed me back my gun. I tucked it into my holster.

"You need any help, Karl, you just yell. Bruno'll hear you and I'll come running."

"You bet, Maude. I'll be sure to do that."

She had her last look at me. "Your show stinks, mister."

Then she vanished, along with her carbine and her dog, into the shadows behind us.

"C'mon inside," Karl Leifer said, waving me across the threshold.

He went across to a rocking chair, picked up a sizable black ear horn, stuck it in his ear and said, "I'll be able to hear you better now. So how can I help you, young man?"

"I'm trying to find out about Evelyn Saunders."

"Oh, yes, nice young woman. Known her since she was a little girl."

"Have you seen her recently?"

He didn't hesitate. "I certainly did. Just this morning, in fact." As he spoke, he looked at an eight-by-ten pale blue envelope on a small table a few feet away. I wondered what had been in the envelope.

"She was on your train?"

"Yes, she was."

"You're sure it was her?"

"I guess I don't know what you're getting at."

"You saw her face-to-face?"

"Why, sure. How else would I see her?"

"I just meant that you actually saw her. Nobody just told you she was on board."

"No, I saw her."

"Did you speak to her?"

"Yes. Asked how her father was doing. He's an ornery old bastard, I know, but we're both Lutherans."

"What did she say?"

"How about you handing me that glass of beer over there?"

"Here you go."

"You want one?"

"No, thanks," I said.

With one hand he sipped his beer. With the other he held his ear horn in place.

"I really should be gettin' to bed. Came out here 'cause I couldn't sleep. Older I get, the more trouble I have sleepin'. Had a pappy just like that. But I really should be headin' for the sack. I gotta get up in a few hours."

"You were telling me about speaking to her."

"Oh. Right."

"Did she seem nervous or anything?"

"Nervous? Hmm." He thought a long moment. "Now that you mention it, I guess she did seem a little bit funny. But it was early in the morning. Most town folks like her, they aren't used to getting up that early."

"Do you know where she was going?"

"Junction City, her ticket said. That's where I get off and come back."

"So she was with you to Junction City?"

He shook his sleek bald head. He looked around the small room, which had a good Sears dining table and a menagerie of railroad paraphernalia on the walls. There were framed photographs of trains, a couple different styles of conductor hats, three or four sizes of conductor whistles, plates and cups and glasses and even a tablecloth from different towns along his Rock Island run, and a painting of one of the robber barons who destroyed several thousand lives building his railroad.

"Nope," Karl Leifer said. "And that's the funny thing."

"What is?"

"Well, I went to say good-bye to her, but she wasn't there."

"You didn't see her leave the train?"

"Nope."

"Could she have left without you seeing her?"

"Don't think so. Anyway, I went up and asked the station man there if he'd seen a young woman get off the train. He'd been out on the platform there since we'd pulled in. He hadn't seen any young woman at all."

"So she got on the train but she didn't leave the train? How is that possible?"

He took out his ear horn. "Damn thing starts to hurt after a while." Took a sip of beer. "All I can figure out is that she got off at Kenyon."

Kenyon was a stop about twelve miles out of Belden City.

"Kenyon? There isn't anything there. Why would she get off there?"

"Young fella, you want answers I can't give you. And you're gettin' kinda prickly in the process."

I smiled. "I guess I am. Sorry."

"She got on the train in Belden City. That much I can vouch for. When we got to Junction City, she wasn't on the train. Or didn't appear to be, anyway. Which means either she got off at Kenyon—and Lord knows I couldn't tell you why she'd do that—or she got off the train at Junction City and we just didn't see her."

With that, he put the horn back in his ear.

"Doesn't make a lot of sense."

He grinned. "You'll notice that the older you get."

"What's that?"

"That things don't make a lot of sense. By my age, almost nothin' makes any sense. You just accept things as they are, and then one day they bury you and none of it matters no more."

I wondered if all Lutherans were this optimistic about things.

"Well, I thank you for your time, Mr. Leifer," I said, standing up. "Sorry for all the commotion."

I went over and shook his hand.

"Hell, don't worry about Maude. She sits by that back door of hers all night, and soon as that damned dog of hers makes a peep, she's outside with her carbine. You made her week, son. She'll be tellin' the neighbors about how she got the drop on that smart-alecky trick shooter from the show downtown."

I laughed. "She didn't seem to think much of my show."

He shrugged. "Well, I don't either, to be perfectly honest, but then I don't pretend to be no critic."

I guess it was a good thing I hadn't offered him any complimentary tickets.

I said good night, went out the back door, walked back across the dewy grass to the sidewalk, Bruno's enraged barking pushing me along, and started back to my room.

Now, I was ready to crawl into bed and get some sleep. I needed to think through what I'd learned at Leifer's. None of it made much sense. Why would she get off at Kenyon? And why did she have a ticket to only Junction City when her father had told me she was going way up the Territory to visit kin?

I was working through all these things when I reached the mouth of an alley about half a block from my boarding-house. I was maybe three steps across the alley when I heard it and maybe five steps across the alley when I felt it.

Somewhere in the darkness somebody with a rifle had taken aim and fired off two quick shots.

One of them got me up high in the right shoulder and spun me around and knocked me to my knees.

I knelt there in shock and anger and confusion and pain while I heard, in the near darkness, the sound of heavy footsteps running away down the packed dirt of the alley-way.

The blood wasn't considerable yet, but the pain sure was.

In the surrounding windows, flickering yellow lantern light could be seen now.

This was the civilized west of 1894. Gunshots in the middle of the night were something that alarmed the local citizenry.

Ghostly faces peered past lace curtains as fearful, curious eyes watched me stagger down the street toward the hospital.

10

The hospital went two floors, ten beds, three nurses and a doctor who smelled of peppermint, meant to disguise the fact that he really smelled of whiskey. Takes one to know one, I guess.

I lay on my back in the surgery while Dr. Snead, a plump hearty man with the face of a cherub and the eyes of a cynical old man, took out the bullet, cleansed the wound, and gave me a brief spiel about how to avoid getting gangrene. He would be typical of the frontier doctor—at least until Jeremiah Belden had built his city this nice new hospital—a man who could pull a tooth, amputate a leg, or, as in my case, take out a bullet.

I tried to imagine Evelyn Saunders in her white uniform standing next to him, smiling at me with her gentle brown eyes.

But it wasn't Evelyn who stood next to him. It was my good friend Sonia Eckstrom, the hard Swedish nurse who'd come to the show yesterday looking for Evelyn.

Sonia did not seem unhappy when I grunted with pain as the doctor's shining silver tools extracted the bullet. Nor did she seem unhappy when I got a little faint and nearly rolled off the padded table. She grabbed me harder than was necessary and sort of slammed me back in place. Hard enough anyway, for the good doctor Snead to shoot her an odd look.

Finished, washing his hands in a white basin a few feet away, he said, in doctorly jest, "I'd say you're going to live, Mr. Coldwell."

I matched his jest. "That won't necessarily come as good news to everybody in this town."

I watched Sonia Eckstrom as I said this. She did not smile.

"Well, we all have our friends and enemies, Mr. Coldwell," the doctor said. "A few years ago a man took a shot at me because he said that I was a warlock and had conspired with his wife to deliver a child who was the anti-Christ."

He turned back to me, wiping his pink plump hands on a clean white towel.

"So you see, there are all kinds of reasons that people dislike other people. The only thing you can worry about is if you're good to the people who care about you. Nobody else matters, the way I see it."

He seemed to suddenly sense the ill will between Sonia Eckstrom and me. He looked at her and smiled. "Wouldn't you agree, Nurse Eckstrom?"

"Yes." One syllable. No feeling. Except for her blue eyes. They were as hard and harsh as ever.

He came over and took one more look at the work he'd done. He might have been a carpenter admiring a cabinet he'd just completed.

"Nice work, if I say so myself. Don't think there's much chance of any gangrene. But remember what I told you to watch for."

"I will, Doctor. And thank you. I appreciate your getting out of bed this late."

"Why don't you lie here now and get some rest? Nobody's using this surgery any more tonight, anyway."

"Thanks."

He glanced at Sonia Eckstrom. "You'll be here to get Mr. Coldwell anything he wants, won't you?"

"Yes, Doctor."

"Good. Well, good night, Mr. Coldwell."

He went over to the door, took another look at each of us, then went quietly away.

Sonia Eckstrom went to work cleaning up after the surgery. She worked quickly, deftly, and with almost mechanical accuracy. She dumped the bloody rags, the tatters of my bloody shirt, the remnants of the cloth the good doctor had made my sling from.

Then she set about straightening cabinets, chairs, and the table I lay on.

As usual, she moved me a lot harder than was strictly necessary. But I wasn't going to give her the satisfaction of complaining. We played our little games, Nurse Eckstrom and me.

"There's some coffee."

"No, thanks," I said.

"Tea, perhaps."

"No, thanks. But water would be good. The colder the better."

I not only felt weak, I also felt a little feverish, chill then warm then chill again. Right now I felt hot.

"Very well."

She went away. I could hear her in the long, empty corridor, her curt steps receding into the midnight gloom of the hospital.

Every few minutes, I'd start wondering who shot me and why. A public drunk always picks up some enemies. But I doubted I'd picked up any enemy who'd want to shoot me. I wasn't important enough to shoot, for one thing.

That left only one other possible reason—the questions

I'd started asking about Evelyn's disappearance. No other reason anybody could possibly want to shoot me.

But why?

Sonia Eckstrom handed me a cool glass of water. "Thanks."

She nodded. Didn't say you're welcome.

She started to leave, and I said, "Who does Evelyn know in Kenyon?"

"Nobody I know of. Why?"

For the first time, her tone was mildly cordial. I realized that she didn't care for me, but she did care, apparently a great deal, for Evelyn. As long as we talked about Evelyn, Sonia would be at least civil if not friendly.

"That's where she got off."

"Off what?"

"The train."

"What train?"

So I told her everything I'd learned. Especially about the part where Evelyn had seemed to leave the train at Kenyon.

Sonia Eckstrom thought a long moment and said, "No, I can't think of anybody she's ever mentioned who lived there." She shook her head. "That seems very strange."

"Yes. Unless she was lured there."

"Lured? By who?"

"A man who blamed her for the death of his son?"

"My Lord, you don't mean Jeremiah Belden, do you?"

"That's exactly who I mean."

"But how would he lure her?"

"I don't know. That's the part I haven't figured out yet."

"You're sure he blamed Evelyn?"

"I was standing right there when he looked down at his dead son in the street and then a few minutes later said that he held Evelyn responsible for this."

"You think he'd kill her?"

"I think it's at least a possibility."

"Maybe you'd better see the marshal."

"What if he's part of it?"

"Part of luring Evelyn?"

I nodded.

"You don't trust many people, do you, Mr. Coldwell?"

"I guess I don't."

I sipped water. I was still feeling hot. I needed to use the bed pan in the corner. I wanted to walk over and get it myself. I didn't want to humiliate myself by asking Nurse Eckstrom here to help me.

"Who do you think shot you?"

"I don't know."

"You can't even guess?"

"Well, obviously it's somebody who doesn't like me asking questions about Evelyn."

"I told you this was unlike her. Rushing off this way, without a word to the hospital."

"You were right, Nurse Eckstrom, and I was wrong. I hope you find that satisfying."

There'd been a little more sarcasm on the last line than I'd intended.

"We don't have to hate each other, Nurse Eckstrom."

"I suppose not. Maybe I was wrong about you."

"And maybe I was wrong about you."

She touched me on the arm of my wounded shoulder. "Maybe you're not such a bad man, after all."

"Now there's a glowing recommendation."

She laughed, and it was a pleasant surprise. Despite her size, she had a little girl's laugh, quick and pure and touching. I wanted to make her laugh again sometime. Her laugh was a great reward.

"You need to rest now. I'll turn down the lamp."

"Thank you."

She went over and took care of the lamp. The room was

shadowy and darkly golden now. She looked younger and sweeter in this light. More like her laugh.

"Would you like any more water?"

"No, thanks."

"I'll check on you in half an hour."

"I'll look forward to it."

"Oh. I should have asked. Do you need to use the bed pan?"

There was the real test of our new friendship. Was I comfortable enough to ask her to do the dirty job of bringing me a bed pan? Only somebody you really cared deeply about should be given a duty like that. Did I care deeply enough about Nurse Eckstrom to have her put her clean Swedish hands on that urine-haunted pan and bring it over to me?

Apparently not.

Though my bladder was getting adamant, I said, "No, I'm fine."

"You sure?"

"I'm sure. But thank you."

She went away again, footsteps down the long dark hall.

I eased myself off the table and wobbled my way over to the bed pan on the counter.

I had just picked up the pan and started to unbutton my trousers when a great black wave overwhelmed me. I felt dizzy and out of breath and shaky in the knees.

I heard myself fall into the counter, heard the metal bed pan fall clanking to the floor.

The sound seemed to fill and echo in every corner of the hospital. If there were any corpses here, I'm sure they had been awakened, too.

Still dizzy as I put out my hand stiff-armed to keep from falling.

Quick certain steps coming back down the hall.

The cool competent hands of Nurse Eckstrom on the warm skin of my arms.

She led me back to the table. Helped me to lie back comfortably.

"I would have brought you the pan."

"I know."

"You men," she said. "You're all little boys." She smiled. "I really don't have this great urge to see your pecker, Mr. Coldwell."

"Well, now I can rest a lot easier."

"Here. I'll set the pan right on your stomach. When you feel well enough to use it, go ahead. Then just call my name and I'll come down the hall and take it from you."

"I appreciate that."

She went away again.

It was a long time before I felt well enough to sit up and drain my bladder.

I stage-whispered her name and she was there in half a minute, taking the pan from me, leaving the room.

I lay back and closed my eyes and wondered about who had tried to kill me.

Just at first light, roosters roaring at the dawn, the first clatter of farm wagons in the dusty streets, Marshal Shay was there, standing by the bed they'd put me in after getting the surgery ready for an early operation.

The room was small and square and white. The pearly dawn gave the walls a certain soft glow. Maybe I'd died and gone to heaven and simply hadn't realized it yet.

But then I realized that heaven probably wouldn't include Marshal Shay, especially not with two good-sized razor nicks on his chin.

"Somebody shot you, Mr. Coldwell."

"That's what I was told."

"You want to tell me about it?"

"Not much to it, really, Marshal."

"I understand that you were at Karl Leifer's house earlier."

"Right."

"Asking questions about Evelyn Saunders."

"Right again."

"I guess I didn't realize that you were a detective, Mr. Coldwell. Are you with Pinkerton or on your own?"

"I'm just one of those people who gets curious when a young woman vanishes that way."

"She didn't vanish, Mr. Coldwell. She got on a train, as I'm sure Karl told you, and she went to visit some relatives."

"Karl also told me she didn't get off at Junction City."

"Well, as you probably noticed, Mr. Coldwell, Karl is also very deaf and his eyesight isn't much better. Karl probably just didn't see her get off."

"Nobody else did, either."

"That early in the morning, a lot of things slip past a person's attention."

I winced at the pain that came and went at quirky intervals.

"Hurt?"

"Sometimes."

He sighed, ran his hat through his fingers. "Why don't you just let it lie?"

"Evelyn, you mean?"

"Evelyn and everything. She's a grown woman. She has a right to do what she wants with her life. If her father isn't worried, why should you be?"

I watched him carefully. I wanted to see how he'd react to what I was about to say. "I think Jeremiah Belden shot me."

He reacted with just enough anger to confirm my suspicions. He knew what was really going on with Evelyn. He was working for Jeremiah Belden. "What the hell are you talking about?"

"Not shot me personally. Jeremiah doesn't do much of anything personally. He hires things done. So I guess I should say I think he had me shot."

"Why would he do a thing like that?"

"Same reason you came over here this morning."

"Which is?"

"Because you want me to stop asking about Evelyn."

Dr. Snead peeked into my room. "How're you doing?"

"I'd like to get some rest, but the marshal here won't let me."

"I thought you were a lot more considerate a man than that, Marshal," Dr. Snead said. "Why don't you leave now and let him rest."

Marshal Shay put his hat on, gave me another one of his looks, and walked out.

"You're looking a little pale this morning," Dr. Snead said when he came in.

"I'm feeling a little pale."

"You rest up here this morning. We'll send you home this afternoon."

"Thanks for helping me get rid of Shay."

He smiled, his fat face cherublike again. "I was just doing my doctorly duty, Mr. Coldwell. Anyway, Shay and I get along fine."

"Oh?"

"Apparently you didn't know."

"Know what?"

"He's my brother-in-law."

With that cheery news, Dr. Snead went about his other doctorly chores.

11

"Are you awake?"

"I wasn't until you asked."

"It's time to go."

"And leave your warm loving presence?"

"I try to be a good nurse."

I looked at Sonia Eckstrom and smiled. "And you do a good job, actually."

"I don't like you when you're sarcastic."

"I don't like me when I'm sarcastic, either."

"My father is like that."

I wasn't going to ask the obvious: Don't you like your father? Instead, I said, "Any word on Evelyn?"

She shook her head. She looked drawn, worried.

"She'll turn up. You'll see," I said.

"Do you really believe that?"

"I'm trying to," I said.

She came over, got me under the arms, helped raise me gently to a sitting position.

"You really are a good nurse."

"Now you're getting carried away with flattery. I'm good, but not remarkable in any way. And there are a lot of good nurses in this country."

The hospital had provided me with a new shirt. She fixed it on me very easily until she got to my cast.

"I'll need your help."

I helped her.

It wasn't easy accommodating the shirt, especially not with all the pain that went along with it, but eventually we got the job done.

"Will you be all right to walk home alone?"

"Fine. No problem."

"You're sure?"

"I'm sure."

"I'd be glad to walk you."

She took my good arm. We walked down the long, freshly waxed corridor to where daylight showed in the panes of the front double doors.

"I saw Jeremiah Belden today," she said. "On the street."

"Oh?"

"I almost couldn't control myself. I almost went up to him and accused him of kidnapping Evelyn."

"I'm glad you didn't."

"Why?"

"Because then he might have to kidnap you. You have to be very careful of Jeremiah. Very careful."

At the door she said, "You weren't as bad a patient as I thought you'd be."

I laughed. "Another glowing recommendation."

She hesitated and then set her jaw in a determined way. "I want to say something to you."

"All right."

"Something that's none of my business."

"Fine."

"Something you have every right to get mad at."

I nodded. "Why don't you just say it?"

"Take a look at your skin in the light sometime."

"My skin?"

"That's one way you can detect early liver trouble."

"Ah. Demon rum."

"Yes, Mr. Coldwell. Demon rum."

"I mean to get around to that someday."

"Those are the last words of a dying drunkard."

"You're very dramatic."

"Have you ever seen anybody die from alcohol, Mr. Coldwell?"

"Guess I haven't."

"It's very ugly and very sad."

I sighed. "I appreciate what you're trying to do, Nurse Eckstrom."

"You do, honestly?"

"Honestly."

She laughed softly. "Good, then there's hope for you yet."

She opened the door for me.

The world waited, clatter of wagon, shouts of kids, whistle of factory starting the next shift.

"You sure you'll be all right to walk?"

"I'll be fine."

"You look a little wobbly. If you want me to be perfectly honest."

"I'm fine, Nurse Eckstrom. If you want me to be perfectly honest."

"Good day, then."

"Good day, Nurse Eckstrom."

And I set off, down the six stairs to the boardwalk, across the boardwalk to the street, down the street to the first hitching rail and—

I dropped.

No prelude. No warning. No big drama.

My legs simply gave out.

She was there in moments.

"Sure you don't want some company, Mr. Coldwell?"

I let her help me up and walk me all the way home.

12

I've never been popular with the other people in my boardinghouse. I'm told that one night when they were all sitting on the front porch, I came weaving down the street, stumbled and banged my head on the dirt roadway, and then threw up all over the man who came down to help me.

Things like that leave an indelible impression on people's minds, and whatever else you might be—generous, amusing, helpful—you'll always be the guy who threw up on his boardinghouse friend. That's all they'll ever remember about you.

The night after I returned from the hospital and sat down to dinner, their attitude changed a little, the five older men who sat around Mrs. Byrnes's table loudly smacking their lips as they ate and letting out tiny explosive belches every few minutes. White-haired Mr. Steivers, who had long suffered a problem with gas, perfumed the air in his usual way. Mr. Barker, another geezer, got gravy on one of Mrs. Byrnes's two good lace tablecloths and suffered the usual penalty, one of Mrs. Byrnes's withering looks of disapproval. If you were having an especially bad day, she might be able to drive you to suicide with that look.

"So you got shot, Coldwell?" Carter said. He was the

youngest man at the table, a kid really, twenty or so, who worked for the railroad. He nodded to my white sling.

"Afraid I did."

"You know who did it?"

"Not yet."

"Think you'll find out?"

"If Marshal Shay takes it seriously, I will."

"Town's goin' to shit," Mr. Steivers-with-the-gas-problem said. "Every day, somebody's gettin' shot."

"This hardly makes us a bad town," said Mrs. Byrnes sternly. "Every place has its troubles once in a while." Not a bad word about Belden City ever passed without Mrs. Byrnes slapping it down and then stepping on it. She was a town supporter of fanatical proportion.

"Personally," said Mills, who wasn't much older than Carter and who worked as a teller at the bank, "I'd find the shooter myself and kill him."

"Kill him?" Mrs. Byrnes said. "Mr. Coldwell didn't die."

"No," said Mills, "but the guy was still a bushwhacker, and bushwhackers should be killed on general principles."

Ordinarily, if I was at the table, they didn't talk much, if at all. When I'd leave, and sit upstairs in my room with the door ajar, I'd hear them not only talking, but laughing. But if I went downstairs again, the conversation always stopped.

But my wound and my sling had made me a human being for at least a night, and even though I'd told myself that I didn't care that they considered me a freak and a geek, I felt good about them including me again tonight.

"I'm goin' up to get a bucket of beer, Coldwell. You want me to get you a bucket?" Carter, the kid, said.

"I'd appreciate that. I'll go upstairs and get you a dime."

"You don't worry about that, Coldwell. Tonight's on me." He looked around the dining room table. "Anybody else want a bucket?"

"Only if you're paying." Mills smiled.

"Tell you what, Mills," Carter said. "You let me shoot you in the arm like Coldwell here got it, and I'll be happy to buy you a bucket."

Everybody laughed.

Carter went out for the buckets and was back in ten minutes. I drank two glasses with him and then left the dining room with its solemn grandfather clock and solemn mahogany furnishings and went up and lay down in my room, still weak from the wound.

I was just sort of drifting off into darkness when I remembered suddenly what the day after tomorrow was, and when I remembered, I felt worse than any gunshot could ever have made me feel.

Two days from now would have been Mac's birthday.

A sorrow took me then, and for a long time I didn't know where I was, or care where I was, or care who I was or what happened to me. There was just Mac's little-boy body lying broken on the carnival grass, and my wife leaning over him and sobbing and sobbing. . . .

I suppose I cried, though not in any dramatic way, just a few warm tears on my cheeks and a terrible deadness in my heart. . . .

And after a while, the last night birds calling to each other in the dying day, I slept a little bit and luckily didn't dream of any little boys being shot to death by their fathers. . . .

When I woke up, the first thing I became aware of was the pain in my shoulder and arm. The second thing I noticed was how dry I was. My first thought was of alcohol, of course, but I would gladly have settled for clean, clear water.

I lay there for a long time, listening to the thunder of the midnight trains in the hills, and the nearer sounds of the boardinghouse—the man coughing in the next room, the bedsprings squeaking as someone heavy tossed and turned, the childlike whimpering of an old man's nightmare.

Rain was on the wind through the window, rain and the quiet smoky sorrow of autumn.

I sat up. Blinding flashes of pain shot up my arm. I could smell my own blood seeping through the bandages. Blood and the poisons being excreted, too, unclean.

I built a cigarette one-handed, feeling ridiculously proud of myself for my achievement, and then I sat on the edge of my bed and stared out the window.

The rain came then, fast and hard at first, then slower and softer.

I knew what I wanted to do, and what I needed to do, I just didn't know if I had the strength.

I stood up.

Or tried to. I was so dizzy, I quickly let myself sink back to the bed.

Cold sweat scalded my hot forehead.

I lay back. My breath came in rushes and gushes and heaves. And even though I tried to fight it, I felt myself slipping back into clammy, sick sleep.

There were no trains in the hills, not the second time I awoke that night. Nor were there any sounds from the adjoining rooms. There was just darkness and stillness and the goose bumps on my arms and legs. Winter was whispering on the night, whispering the icy promise of soon, soon.

In the next ten minutes I accomplished three things: I stood up without falling back down; I got my clothes on; and I located and successfully strapped on my gun belt.

I left the room. The stairs leading down were steep and dark, and I leaned against the wall for support all the way.

And that was when I tripped over the spittoon that Mrs. Byrne kept next to the hat tree in the vestibule.

The response to the clang and clatter was immediate.

I heard Mrs. Byrnes, or the Widow Byrnes, as she was more often called, ease from her downstairs bed and slap quickly across the floor in bare feet.

In moments she flung her apartment door back and stood there in a flannel nightshirt, looking purposeful and grim in the light of the lantern she carried.

Oh, yes, and in the other hand she held a sawed-off shotgun that looked as if it could intimidate even the most fearless of men.

"What the Sam Hill are you doing up at this hour?" Mrs. Byrnes said.

"Going for a walk," I said.

She sniffed at me, as if trying to determine if there was liquor on my breath, and then gave up. "A walk? My gosh, son, don't you know what time it is?"

"I couldn't sleep."

"So you had to wake everybody up?"

"Mrs. Byrnes?" a groggy male voice called from the top of the stairs. "Is everything all right down there?"

"You go back to sleep, Lumere. Everything's fine."

"What is it?" the old man wanted to know.

"Just Mr. Coldwell. Going out for a walk."

"A walk? Don't he know what time it is?"

"Well, if he didn't before, he does now," Mrs. Byrne said.

"He's a crazy sonofabitch, that Coldwell is."

"You go back to sleep now, Lumere."

"A crazy sonofabitch if I ever saw one," Lumere said.

Then it was *his* bare feet slapping the bare floor as he returned to his room.

"You want some help back upstairs?" Mrs. Byrnes said.

"I'm not going back upstairs, Mrs. Byrnes."

"Son, I think you're getting fevered or something. This just don't make sense, going out at this hour."

"I'll be fine."

"The way you were fine when you tripped over the spittoon."

"An accident was all, Mrs. Byrnes. Just an accident."

I started toward the front door.

"I sure hope you know what you're doing," Mrs. Byrnes said behind me.

I laughed. "I sure hope I do, too."

13

Just before dawn the grass in the park was heavy with dew. A stray hound rummaged among some underbrush, eventually causing a rabbit to come sprinting out to safety. The way the underbrush rustled, you might have expected a buffalo to come racing out.

The bench where Evelyn and I usually sat was damp. I wiped it off and sat down. By my railroad watch, I still had forty minutes to go before I went over to Bob Saunders's house. He wouldn't leave for work till dawn. He worked at the local wagon works. The shift started there at six A.M.

I smoked two cigarettes, once again made with great dexterity by the Amazing Coldwell, and I went through everything once again.

It didn't make any more sense than it had yesterday. There was just no reason for Evelyn to leave town the way she supposedly had.

He came out at 5:47, a small bundled-up man walking fast toward Main Street.

If I went in any later, with any more light in the sky, a neighbor was sure to see me.

I moved across the street, along the side of his small house, to the back door.

Across the alley and up a slight incline, I saw lantern light in one of the windows.

I had to work fast.

The window was no problem to jimmy open. The problem was climbing through with my arm in a sling. It took a few awkward, sweaty minutes.

The house smelled of bitter coffee, lamp kerosene, and sleep.

Evelyn's room was directly off the living area. I found nothing disturbed there. Sachet was on the air, her pinafores and blouses were neatly hung in the closet along with two fancy dresses for church and festivities, and four small pairs of shoes were lined against the back wall. None of her nursing clothes were there, but I wasn't sure what that meant.

No sign of her being dragged out of here. No sign that she'd taken much with her on her train trip, if she'd taken anything at all.

I next tried the much smaller room where her father slept amidst a stack of *Police Gazette*s and burned-out pipes and a loving photograph of his dead wife. Seeing the photograph there, thinking of what it probably meant to him, I reasoned that he was probably a more decent man than I'd given him credit for.

That sentiment ended as soon as I started going through his bureau drawers. In the bottom drawer I found a pale blue eight-by-ten envelope. The second one I'd seen recently. This one looked to be full.

After opening it and looking inside, I whistled to myself, closed the envelope and stuck it under my arm.

I was just leaving his bedroom when I heard something outside the house.

I hugged the wall. My heart was loud and fast in my chest now. The cold slick sweats had once more covered my body.

"You're sure you saw somebody go in there?" a male voice said.

"Positive," a female voice said.

"And you're sure it wasn't Saunders?"

The woman speaking presumably belonged to the house across the alley. The man was Marshal Shay.

"Why would Saunders be crawling in his own back window?" the woman said.

"Maybe he forgot his key."

"You afraid to go in there or something, Marshal?"

"I just want to be sure what I'm dealing with here." But he'd taken her words as a challenge to his authority and manhood. "You stand back now, hear?"

"You goin' in?"

"You never mind what I'm going to do. You just stand back."

"Yessir."

Even without his arm in a sling, Shay didn't sound as if climbing through the window was much easier for him. You could hear tobacco and whiskey shortening his breath.

There was only one chance for escape.

Moments before I heard Shay's feet touch the kitchen floor, I bolted for the front door.

It was locked and took me a few frantic moments to unlock it with my one good hand.

As I pushed the screen door open, I heard Shay shout, "You stop right there!"

But I didn't, I went blind running into the dusty street, running faster than I would have thought possible, right down the center of the road, right toward the huge yellow sun just now cresting the silhouette of ragged forest on the hills surrounding this side of town.

Birds and dogs and sleepy humans were just now coming full awake.

Two blocks away I found an alley and took it. I hadn't slowed down. I didn't dare.

Somewhere behind me Shay's voice had now been joined by others, men forming a quick, eager posse. Nothing a man loved more than hunting another man, especially when the law gave him the authority.

Footfalls were loud but turning now in the opposite direction. Shouts and threats came tumbling from raspy morning throats, but were aimed at places where I'd not been and did not plan to be.

I hid in a leaning old barn that smelled of axle grease and dead rotting mice until I was sure it was safe to walk the remaining three blocks to Mrs. Byrnes's boardinghouse.

I went up the back way, so I wouldn't be forced to explain anything to anybody.

I lay shivering in my own sweat, my entire body trembling with exhaustion, the envelope I'd taken from Saunders pushed under the bed.

After a long sleep, and a bath, and some food, I was going to look Saunders up again.

We were going to have ourselves a nice little talk.

14

Neville was there then, in my sleeping room, sitting in a straight-backed chair across from me, playing with his pipe.

"I'm not supposed to have anybody up here," I said, yawning, slow and dopey with sleep.

"I think that only applies to young girls."

"Ah. I should've figured it was something like that." Then I said, "Shit."

"Lot of pain?"

"Lot."

I lay there for a time. There was a breeze. I daydreamed of being someplace far away, much younger and smarter and kinder and luckier, one of those South Sea islands, I suppose, where everybody wants to escape to today.

"There was some excitement this morning."

"Oh?"

Neville nodded. He wore his frock coat but not his top hat. In daylight he looked sad and old without his hat. "Seems somebody broke into Saunders's house."

"Oh."

"Trying to steal something, I suppose."

"I'll be darned."

"You're a lousy bullshit artist, Mitch. You always were."

"You think I broke in there?"

"Hell, yes."

I stayed quiet again. I tried hard to pretend I didn't ache.

"You're not in any condition to get messed up in anything, Mitch."

"I appreciate the concern, John, I really do."

"I'm just being selfish."

"Oh?"

"You're the only one who'll put up with me. I've got to keep you out of trouble, son."

"I think Jeremiah took Evelyn."

"Jeremiah being Jeremiah, you'd have one hell of a time proving that."

"But I think I can prove it."

"You do, really?"

I nodded. Grimaced again.

"Mitch?"

"Yeah."

"You're pushing pretty hard."

"I know."

"And maybe you're wrong."

"Wrong?"

"Maybe Evelyn just took off on her own."

"That'd be one hell of a coincidence, don't you think?"

"Coincidences happen that way sometimes, Mitch."

The pain again, the one straight up my arm and into my shoulder.

"And if you're right, Mitch—"

I looked over at him. "And if I'm right?"

"If you're right, then ol' Jeremiah will kill you. It'll look like an accident, the way ol' Jeremiah always makes everything look like an accident, but you'll be dead all the same."

"I love her."

"I know."

"I didn't think I'd ever love anybody again."

"I'm sorry, Mitch."

"So I've got to keep looking."

"I just needed to say these things."

"I appreciate it."

"I knew you'd tell me to go fuck myself, but I had to say them anyway."

"I didn't tell you to go fuck yourself, John."

"Pretty much, you did."

I laughed. "Well, pretty much I guess you're right."

"You want me to get the Widow Byrnes up here and have her give you an enema or anything?"

"Very funny."

He stood up. Put his top hat on. Ten full years younger he looked. "I can look after the show."

"I'd appreciate it."

"I don't want to see you get all shot up, kid. Or all heart-broken."

"I'll be all right."

"You're a thick-headed sonofabitch, you know that?"

"Yeah," I said, "I guess I am at that."

Then he was just footsteps down the long stairs, and a screen door banging, and a man for the neighbor dog to start barking at all the way down the street.

I got myself some more sleep, sleep filled with troubling dreams whose particulars vanished when I awakened.

All I had left was this deep-down scared feeling, the way I sometimes got when I was young and couldn't find my little brother or sister when a bad thunderstorm was coming.

15

I was back there at four-thirty that afternoon, Saunders's large envelope stuffed inside my jacket.

I saw him through the front window as I came up the walk. The day was ending already, the chill from the mountains in the valley now, a streaky sunset the color of coral making the shabby little house look a lot better than it should have.

One little boy pulling his sister in a wagon took a long, suspicious look at me. A lawman in the making.

As I waited for Saunders to appear, I thought again how lucky I'd been. Nobody, not even Marshal Shay, had recognized me as I was running away this morning. Not even with my arm in a sling.

He peeked out through the lace curtains, saw who it was, leaned back so I couldn't see him.

I took the envelope from inside my jacket and showed it to him.

He was at the front door in moments, flinging it open. "You sonofabitchin' robber."

"Unless you want your neighbors to know what you did, Saunders, you'd better keep your voice down and invite me in so we can have a talk."

"You sonofabitch."

"You said that already."

"You bastard."

"Knock off the crap, Pops, and let me in."

"I should kick your ass, Coldwell."

"Even one-handed, Pops, I could slap you around. Now do what I say. Let me in."

He looked as if he were about to launch another epithet, but then decided against it.

I went inside. He'd been making himself some supper. Something greasy and smelly.

The house was a mess. He'd obviously been searching everywhere for the envelope.

"Sit down over there."

"Nobody comes in here and bosses *me* around."

"I do. Now go over there and sit down in that chair."

"You sonofabitch."

"The names are getting a little old, Saunders. Anyway, we're wasting time." I took the envelope from my jacket and waved it at him.

He said something under his breath, but reluctantly sat down in the chair.

I sat in the rocker across from him.

Sitting down felt better than I wanted to admit. I was still pretty weak from the gunshot.

"There's two thousand dollars in this envelope."

"No shit?" he said.

"Where'd you get it?"

"I don't remember."

"You sold your own daughter for it."

"Stepdaughter."

"What?"

"Evelyn doesn't know it, but I'm not her real old man." Saunders smiled. "Her real old man got himself shot in a whorehouse one night outside of Omaha. Evelyn's mother came out here. She never did tell Evelyn the truth."

Now it made a little more sense. Selling your own daughter was something that was just about unimaginable to me. But selling your stepdaughter . . . Well, that was just within the realm of possibility.

"So you sold her."

"I don't know what you're talking about."

"Sure you don't."

"I came by that money fair and square."

"Oh?"

"Sold a parcel of land I owned."

"Two thousand dollars is a lot of land. Where is this parcel?"

"I don't have to answer your questions."

"You know where Evelyn is, don't you, Saunders?"

"Nope, I don't."

"That's where you got this money, isn't it?"

"I don't know what you're talking about."

I surprised both of us by moving so quickly. In moments I had him by the front of his shirt and was slamming his head against the wall. All with one hand.

"Where is she?"

"I don't know."

"You bastard," I said. "You tell me or I'll keep hitting your head."

I gave him a couple of especially hard shoves to make my point. He started to whimper, plead.

"Put him down, Coldwell."

I'd been so occupied with Saunders that I hadn't heard Shay come in.

I glanced over my shoulder and saw the marshal standing there with a Navy Colt aimed right at my shoulder blade.

"Did you hear me, Coldwell?"

I let Saunders go and turned to face the lawman.

"I came over here to see if Saunders might have remembered anything more about what his robber this morning might have taken."

"Guess I didn't hear about any robbery," I said.

"Sure you didn't, Coldwell. What were you doing about dawn?"

"Sleeping."

"I asked Mrs. Byrnes. She said you left the house just before five."

"Guess I forgot about that."

"Where'd you go?"

"For a walk."

"Where?"

"Along the river."

"Alone?"

"Uh-huh."

"Anybody see you?"

"Huh-uh."

"You're a real bullshit artist, Coldwell. A soak and a bullshit artist. A real nice combination." He looked at Saunders. "What's going on here?"

Saunders looked at me. Then back to Shay. "Nothing. We just had a disagreement."

"About what?"

"I told him I didn't want him meetin' Evelyn no more along the river. When she gets back, I mean."

"So he started slamming you against the wall?"

"That's just what he did, Marshal."

Shay looked at me and smiled. "Guess you're a little tougher than I would have thought, Coldwell, with just one arm and all." The smile went quickly. "This is all a bunch of bullshit and you two know it." He looked at Saunders first and then at me. "I don't know what the hell's going on here, but I'm going to find out."

What was going on here? I wondered. Was Shay just

pretending to know nothing of Evelyn's disappearance—or was he really innocent?

The marshal walked over to the front door, stared at us some more, shook his head and left.

Saunders said, "I want my envelope back."

"You'll get it back if you tell me the truth about Evelyn."

"That's my money."

I patted my jacket, the money beneath. "Why don't you try and take it from me, Saunders."

"You sonofabitch."

"We're back to that again, huh?"

I went over to the door the same way Shay had, and stood there with it open an inch or two just looking at Saunders, the way Shay had at both of us, and then I shook my head.

"She may not be your real daughter, Saunders, but she was stupid to love you and trust you."

Then I slammed my way out of there.

16

Mrs. Byrnes waited until her other boarders had finished their dinner, paying her her usual and well-deserved compliments, before raising the subject.

"The marshall was here," she said.

"I know."

"Asking questions."

"Right."

"Questions I had to answer, Mr. Coldwell."

"I understand."

"I'm a good citizen. Law-abiding."

I looked at her and smiled. "So am I, Mrs. Byrnes, at least most of the time."

"I hope I didn't get you into any trouble."

"I got myself into trouble, Mrs. Byrnes. Nobody else."

"I was worried he was going to take you off to jail or something."

"I appreciate you being worried, Mrs. Byrnes."

"How's your shoulder?"

"Better than I would have thought."

"I don't see you wincing as much."

"Those pills the doc gave me help a lot."

She was silent for a moment. Then, "Mr. Coldwell, I know you've had a difficult life. With your son and all."

I didn't say anything. Just watched her.

"Are you a religious man, Mr. Coldwell?"

"I'd have to say no, I guess."

"Then I'm sure you won't mind that I went to St. Michael's today, right after the marshal left, and lit two votive candles for you."

"I appreciate that."

"A red one and a blue one."

"Thank you very much."

"And then I said a rosary and a novena that you wouldn't get in any trouble."

"That's very decent of you, Mrs. Byrnes."

"And then I got a holy card with St. Christopher on it. He's the patron saint of lost travelers, Mr. Coldwell. And that's what you've been ever since your son was killed. A lost traveler, Mr. Coldwell. I hope you don't mind my saying that."

"Not at all, Mrs. Byrnes. I suspect it's the truth."

"It's just that you remind me so much of my own son, Mr. Coldwell, the only child I ever had, and him being killed in a train wreck and all and—"

She fell to sobbing. She was mourning her son by mourning me, and I felt touched by her sweetness. It's good for each of us to be reminded that there are still people like Mrs. Byrnes in the world. Keeps us from thinking that everybody who walks on two legs is mean and selfish and treacherous.

I went over to her and stood her up and took her to me and held her and let her cry and say her boy's name over and over and over, DeWayne it was, DeWayne, DeWayne, DeWayne, and then she buried her face in my shoulder and cried even harder, and then she eased away from me and put her worn fingers to her teary face, looking sad and young and old and dazed, and then she ran off to the kitchen to hide, embarrassed suddenly.

* * *

This time I went in on the east side of Karl Leifer's small house, so the dog next door wouldn't get as good a chance to see me. Nor would his neighbor Maude have cause to draw her rifle.

I had spent twenty minutes crouching in the alley, waiting to make as sure as I could that nobody was home in the small cottage.

I went in through a side window, jimmying it as usual, hoisting myself and pushing myself through with difficulty.

There wasn't much to search so I was able to cover the house in less than ten minutes. I found exactly what I'd been looking for.

My next search was for something very different. When I found it, I grabbed a glass and went over and sat at the small dining table that faced the front door.

I congratulated myself, told myself that most nights I'd be drunk by now. Thanks to Evelyn's urging, I'd gone from falling-down drunk every night to tapering off, being really drunk only a few hours in the early evening. Now I was taking my first drink of the day. I still wasn't ready to go Evelyn's twenty-four hours dry, but maybe I was getting there.

I took out my long Colt and set it on the table and sat there in the darkness waiting for him.

Given how early he had to get up every morning, I figured he wouldn't be out too late.

Half an hour later he came through the front door, leaned over and deftly lit the oil lamp, and then he turned around facing the back of the house and saw me.

"You're one hell of a good liar, Leifer. One hell of a good one. That ear horn is a nice touch. Makes people think you're a little addled."

"You like the ear horn, huh?" He grinned. "I find it useful sometimes."

"Where is she?"

"You like that sour mash? Friend of mine brought it up from Kentucky."

"You're not deaf, Leifer. Where is she?"

He came over to the table, set the lamp down, pulled a chair out and sat down. "Mind if I take a slug from the bottle?"

"It's your bottle."

"And I should tell you, that gun of yours on the table there doesn't scare me."

"No?"

"You're a decent man, Coldwell. You're a rummy and all, but you're still decent. You'd never shoot some old fart like me."

"Sure I would. If I had to."

He looked at me a long moment then reached over and picked up the bottle of sour mash. The whiskey inside the bottle gurgled as he slugged some down. His bald head shone in the lamplight.

He said, "I take it you mean Evelyn."

"Right."

"Afraid I can't help you."

I patted the large envelope I'd taken from his small roll-top desk. "They didn't give you all this money just because they like you."

"No, they gave it to me to lie."

"About her being on the train?"

"Sure. What else?"

"She wasn't on the train yesterday morning?"

"Not that I know of."

"You really are one hell of a good liar."

He grinned again. "That's because people think I'm too old and slow to lie. They think that when the legs slow down, so does the brain. People are dumb bastards."

"Where is she?"

"I don't have no idea whatsoever, Coldwell. Hell, why would they tell me a thing like that?"

He had some more whiskey. "I don't even know who paid me the money."

"Bullshit."

"I know it sounds like bullshit, but it isn't. Got home last night and the envelope was sittin' here along with a note."

"You still have the note?"

"Nope. Threw it away."

"Of course."

"Now this time, Coldwell, I'm not bullshitting you at all. But you're not believing me."

"So what did this note have to say?"

"Well, it said that I could keep the money if I'd tell anybody who asked that I'd seen Evelyn Saunders on the train yesterday."

"You didn't turn it over to Marshal Shay?"

"I thought about it, Coldwell, I really did. I was raised a strict Lutheran and I do mean strict, my pa would slap my ass for the least little thing I ever did, but I decided what the hell, I ain't gonna have no money when I retire next year. A thousand dollars is gonna help a lot."

"You know the terrible thing?"

"What?"

"I believe you," I said.

He laughed. "Even without my ear horn?"

"Especially without your ear horn."

I poured myself some more of his whiskey. Drank a little. "What's going on here, you think?"

He shrugged. "Don't know. Though I guess I've got a suspicion."

"Oh?"

"Belden's pissed at Evelyn because he thinks she caused all the trouble leading to young Belden killing that man."

"That's how I see this, too."

"But Belden can't just have her killed," he said. "One reason he's managed to stay in power is that he doesn't ever cross the line. And killing Evelyn would definitely be crossing the line."

"So he has her killed but he makes it look as if she just took off?"

Leifer nodded. "Sure. That way, how could you prove he had anything to do with it?"

"Especially with two people, you and her father, insisting that she left town early one morning."

"Guilty as charged," he said.

"And eventually, everybody in town forgets about Evelyn."

"That's how I read all this." He pushed me the bottle.

"No thanks," I said. "I've had my daily dose. Two shots is all."

"I'm impressed. Pretty soon you'll be joining the Salvation Army and pounding that big drum of theirs."

I stood up, a little wobbly from pain, inertia, and whiskey.

"You all right, Coldwell?"

"I think so."

"You don't sound real sure."

"I guess I'm not real sure about anything, including my own health."

"You'll be fine. As long as Belden doesn't put a couple of bullets in your back."

I tapped my sling. "He's already tried."

"Knowing Belden, he'll try again."

I walked to the front door. "That ear horn of yours, that damned thing really does the trick. I figured you for some dumb old bastard for sure."

"I appreciate the sentiments."

I laughed. I didn't want to—in his way he was a part of the whole conspiracy, Leifer was—but I couldn't help myself. He was a ballsy old fart, and an amusing one at that.

17

I was passing the Wild West show when I saw John Neville standing out front, thumbs hooked in his vest pockets, top hat tilted dangerously low. He was obviously drinking. As if I had any right to object.

"Evening, John."

He had been so caught up in his thoughts that at first he didn't seem to recognize me.

"Ah, Mitch, I was just thinking about you."

"Good thoughts, I hope."

He slid his arm around me. Now I knew for sure he was drinking. Neither of us were what you'd call physical.

"You know what I was doing?"

"I guess not."

"I was standing here and imagining what the show would look like if old Jeremiah would just give us a little bit of money to fix it up."

"It'd look pretty good," I said. Then, "But John, I'm in a hurry."

"I could tell."

"You could?"

"Even with your arm in a sling, even with all your pain, you're still agitated, still determined to prove that Jeremiah Belden did something with Evelyn."

102

"I owe her that."

But he had rolled back into his own thoughts again. We stood in the cool autumn night, prairie stars low and brilliant, looking at the shabby show.

"You know the first thing I'd do?"

I decided to give him a minute or two. Wouldn't hurt anything.

"What's the first thing you would do?"

"Right above the ticket booth, here?"

"Uh-huh."

"I'd put a man in full warrior dress. Apache'd probably be the best."

"And then what?"

He began strolling, then, his arm looser on my shoulder now but still there, walking me up and down the front of the tattered old show as if I were his son.

"Well, see over there?"

"In the corner?"

"Pre-cisely. You know what I'd put there?"

"No, what?"

"I'd put a beautiful Indian maid."

"How come?"

"How come? Because beautiful girls make little boys and their fathers crazy. If the Indian warrior didn't snag 'em at first, then the Indian princess would when they drifted down here."

"That's a pretty good plan."

"And then you know what?"

"What?"

"We paint everything white and hire that illustrator from *Wild West Weekly*—Siddons is his name, I think—to paint us all new pictures on the canvas outside the show."

"He'd be pretty expensive, wouldn't he?"

"Yeah, but if we told him what we had in mind, how we

wanted to have the best darned Wild West show anywhere
in the United States—I'll bet he'd do it for us."

He was dreaming, and what was the harm?

"You know, I think you're right, John. I think if we
could present it in just the right way—"

"Hell, yes, if we presented it in just the right way, he'd
be glad to do it for us. We could tell him we'd pay him his
full price after the show really got rolling."

"What about Jeremiah?"

"Buy him out."

"Really?"

"Sure, if we could get the likes of Siddons to help us,
why would we need Jeremiah?"

"That's a good point."

And right then he did it—he'd just been waiting his moment, the old sonofabitch—sort of pretended as if he was
pitching forward, and then his hand shot out and reached
for my .45 and—

"I don't want you to have this, Mitch."

"What the hell're you talking about, John? Give me that
damned gun back."

"I'm hearing a lot of stories."

"Stories? I don't know what you're talking about."

"Jeremiah knows you've been doing a lot of snooping
around and he's not happy. In fact, he's downright pissed
off."

"Give me the gun, John."

But he held it up high. He was four inches taller than I
was anyway, and with my arm and shoulder, I wasn't doing
a lot of stretching.

"You just go home and get some rest, Mitch. You hear
me?"

"John, I want you to give me the gun."

"You just do what I say," he said, still keeping the gun
from my reach.

I hit him harder than I intended, hard enough that he doubled over and vomited up the liquor he'd been drinking all night.

"Aw, shit, John," I said, holding onto his shoulder while he puked. "I'm sorry I hit you that hard."

But he was angry and embarrassed and sick now. When he finished being sick, he stood up, wiping his sleeve across his mouth.

"Here's your fucking gun, Mitch. Next time you want to get your ass shot off, don't expect me to try and stop you."

And with that he walked over to the cabin where he slept nights, making sure to bang the door closed as hard as he could.

"Fucking asshole!" I heard him shout through the window.

I had a pretty good idea who he was talking about.

18

The thing is, the grave doesn't even belong to my son.

One day, walking, I came up and sat on the hill of the graveyard because it looked peaceful, and that was when I saw the stone that read:

TOM CASSIDY
1882–1891
May the Angels Take Him Home

And I started praying to him, or talking to him, or whatever you want to call it, and hoping I could use him as a sort of conduit to my own boy.

So now, couple nights a week, I always stopped up on the hill and knelt in the buffalo grass and spoke my piece.

Maybe it's all bullshit, all the religion we're taught—in fact, if I had to bet, I'd say that it surely is bullshit—but maybe it's all right anyway, maybe just in imagining God we create him, and in creating him make ourselves act a little more charitably most of the time.

Anyway, I said my hello to Tom and told him everything that had been going on with Evelyn and Jeremiah, and I asked him if he'd talked to Mac the past couple of days,

and asked if he'd told Mac that I hadn't forgotten his birthday.

Then there were just the jays and owls and wrens on the
night, and the distant din of town, all whore laughter and
rotgut talk, and I said good night to Tom and wandered on
down from the hill toward the lights and the noise.

I still wanted to talk to Jeremiah.

Even if, I felt pretty sure, Jeremiah didn't want to talk to
me.

As I walked, I tried not to think of John Neville's warning, of how Jeremiah wouldn't appreciate me pressing into
his business this way . . .

And how people who did press into his business just naturally seemed to have all these accidents. . . .

19

Jeremiah Belden was standing at the back of the casino talking to one of the faro dealers when I came in through the bat-wing doors.

The place was quiet tonight, like it was most Sundays. On Friday—which was payday at most of the places in town—never mind that the money should go to the wife and kids, the casino would be booming again.

He saw me, stared at me a long moment, and then went back to talking to the faro man.

The bartender, a hearty man named Bill, waggled a fifth of good whiskey at me. I shook my head. He looked genuinely surprised.

I walked back through the noise of the slapping poker cards, the smells of cigarette smoke and alcohol and dance girl perfume, and the glare and smirks of the locals who regarded me as little more than a joke.

I waited just on the edge of Belden's hearing, just so he had to lower his voice to finish his saying, just so he wouldn't forget I was there.

When he finished and the faro dealer said all the usual ass-kissy things a man like Belden expected to hear, he looked over at me and said, "Shame about your shoulder. Being shot and all."

"You sound real sorry."

"You forget, Mr. Coldwell, I have an investment in you. Without you, the Belden Family Wild West Spectacular would be out of business." He tipped his cigar in the direction of my sling. "Every day that sling of yours is on, I lose money. So, you see, I really do wish you a speedy recovery."

"You took her, didn't you?"

"I beg your pardon?"

"Evelyn Saunders. You took her somewhere, didn't you?"

The dark eyes got hard. A petulance touched the lips. "Maybe you don't give a shit about such things, Mr. Coldwell, but I lost my one and only child about forty-eight hours ago. Now most people, even people who don't care about me at all, are polite enough to be pleasant to me during my mourning period."

It wasn't his usual tough-guy talk. His eyes were starting to tear up and there was a waver in his voice.

"I lost my fucking son, Coldwell," he said, angry now. "If anybody should know what I'm going through, you should."

And I couldn't help myself. I wanted to hate him for who he was and what he was, but at that moment he was just a father, the way I was just a father, and I felt his loss and grief and frenzy, and so I just let him turn around and walk away, back to the things he owned and controlled, things that never died on him unless he wanted them to.

As I worked my way back toward the bat-wing doors, the smell of sour mash was tempting.

I walked fast, right out through the doors.

Three blocks from the casino, I ran into the naked man. Or rather, he ran into me.

He was running from an alley, turning right, and there I was.

Being heavier by thirty pounds, I stood still while he bounced away and nearly went over backward, his skinny arms windmilling, little desperate grunts escaping his lips.

This was the infamous Mr. Blackemore I'd met the other night when his keepers from the Brooks House had been chasing him down the street.

He sure had an affinity for cold weather, this scrawny, white-haired, sixty-year-old lunatic standing before me. He wasn't even shivering. It couldn't have been much more than thirty degrees.

He smelled as good as ever, of sweat and urine and vague sickness.

"They're after me," Blackemore said, crazy as ever.

"I imagine they are, Mr. Blackmore, if you mean the people from the Brooks House. You scare them when you run off this way."

"They put snakes in my room." He said this as a wild-eyed accusation, one that sprayed spittle into the air.

Not often, I thought, that I stood in the middle of the street talking to a naked old escapee from an asylum. Probably wasn't going to do my reputation any good.

"And that's not all."

"No?"

"Sure ain't, young fella. They put snakes in my bed and lizards in my closet."

"Lizards?"

"Green slimy ones that attack me in the middle of the night. And then you know what?"

"Uh-uh."

"Then when I tell my friends there about the snakes and the lizards, you know what happens?"

"What happens?"

"They don't believe me."

"You need to calm down, Mr. Blackemore."

"And they're supposed to be my friends."

I was going to suggest that he wait there, while I went and looked for the asylum guards, but I knew better. The moment I left, he'd take off running again.

"She's nice to me."

"Good, Mr. Blackemore, I'm glad you've got a friend."

I was looking up and down the street for any sign of the Brooks House guards.

"She's upstairs. As high as you can go."

"Well, I hope she's comfortable."

"Oh, she's probably comfortable all right, but I'm just afraid she'll get lonely. Nobody to talk to."

"Yeah, she probably does," I said, muttering as my eyes kept scanning alleys and the street. Where were his guards?

"Her being a nurse and all," he said.

The funny thing was, it didn't register at first. Her being a nurse and all. I kept looking for his guards. And then, as if somebody had thrown a switch, his meaning filled my head.

"You said nurse?"

"That's what I said, young fella."

"And you said she's young."

"Young and pretty."

"When did she come there?"

"Other night."

"Mr. Blackemore?"

"Uh-huh."

"I want you to concentrate real hard for me. Can you do that?"

"I guess so."

"Concentrate real hard and listen very carefully to what I ask you. All right?"

"I'll sure give it a try."

"Do you remember me from the other night?"

"The other night?"

"You snuck out of the Brooks House and ran to town here. You were running down the middle of the street when you saw a young woman and me. Does that sound familiar to you?"

"I guess so."

But from his glazed eyes and dazed voice, I could tell that he had no idea what I was talking about.

And then I heard the slapping footfalls, coming fast.

Only yards away now, the guards, closer, closer.

"Mr. Blackemore, is the nurse the same woman you saw with me the other night?"

But it was too late. Mr. Blackemore still looked dazed. And his guards were just a few feet away.

Tears filled his pale blue eyes; his hands made mincing little flights to his face, as if he thought I might hit him.

"Please, Mr. Blackemore, tell me."

"I think so. I think she's the one."

Seeing how much I'd upset him, seeing what a decent old bastard he was, I said, "It's all right, Mr. Blackemore. Just calm down now."

"Here you are, Mr. Blackemore," said one of the guards. "You sure gave us a chase tonight."

Mr. Blackemore whinnied. "I coulda gotten all the way to the county line if this here fella hadn't stopped me."

"Much obliged," said the guard.

"He sure gets out a lot," I said.

"Yeah, and the funny thing is, we can't figure out how he's doing it."

"This is the one that puts the snakes in my room," Mr. Blackemore said, nodding to the first guard, the one with the bowler.

"Yes," said the one with the Stetson, "and I'm the one that puts the lizards in your closet."

"See? See? I told ya they was doin' that," Mr. Blackemore said to me.

They smiled at me and took him away.

He waved, all sad now and scared, fighting them a little with his scrawny dying body, and when they started taking him around the corner, he glanced back at me, beseeching he was, wanting some sort of help I couldn't give him.

I was drained suddenly, and the pain was back in my shoulder and arm.

I went home and slept.

20

She was on her way to work, was Sonia Eckstrom, the next day, and I fell into step beside her.

The autumn morning was blue of sky and chill of air and bright of sunlight. The last leaves burned bright in their fever; there was beauty in the dying.

Roosters and dogs and cawing crows accompanied us.

She still looked sleepy, the big blonde woman, and the sleepiness gave her face a softness it normally lacked. She was dressed in white, taking long, purposeful nurse steps as we headed down the plank sidewalk to the hospital.

After a few pleasantries, which did not seem to interest her unduly, I said, "I think I know where Evelyn is."

She stopped. "Where?"

"The Brooks House."

"The Brooks House? Why would she be in an asylum?"

"That's where Jeremiah Belden wants her. Why, I'm not sure yet."

She began walking again.

"Did I say something to make you mad?" I said, walking along with her.

"That's a pretty crazy story, Mr. Coldwell."

"I know it is. But it's true."

"I need to ask you something, Mr. Coldwell."

The other night in the hospital, after the bed pan humor we'd shared, I'd sensed that she was starting to accept me a little. Now, I didn't have that sense at all.

"All right," I said. "Ask me."

"Were you drinking heavily last night?"

"This isn't something I hallucinated, Sonia."

"So somebody told you this?"

We had to pause on the street to let a stagecoach clatter through. There was still a short-run stage in service in this part of the Territory.

The stagecoach was followed by three dour Shawnee elders wearing white man's flannel shirts. The Shawnee had recently lost a court battle over some land. These three Shawnee looked as if they were bearing the entire emotional burden themselves.

"Indians," she said. "I'll just never like them."

I shrugged. "I'm not crazy about them, I guess, but they're people just like us."

She gave me a look that said they weren't people like us at all. Least ways, not people like her and her Scandinavian kin.

We were three blocks from the hospital. I hadn't even raised the subject of why I was up so early trailing her to work.

I answered the question she'd last asked. "Somebody who should know told me about Evelyn."

"And who would that be?"

I realized then that I couldn't tell her the exact truth. I couldn't say, Well, I was walking home the other night when this naked man came running down the street, afraid that these two guards would capture him and bring him back to the asylum and start putting snakes in his room and lizards in his closet.

Now there was a reliable witness.

"Somebody associated with the Brooks House," I said.

"He's seen her there? Evelyn, I mean?"

I guess he hadn't actually said that he'd seen her for himself. Not exactly. "He knows she's there. He's positive."

"If you really believe this, why are you wasting time with me? Why aren't you at the marshal's?"

"Because I don't know if I can trust him."

"You think he knows where Evelyn is?"

"I think that's a possibility."

"Then what do you plan to do?"

The hospital was half a block away. I didn't have much time to make my pitch.

"When the marshal can't handle drunks, what happens to them?" I said.

"Well, we take them. If they're in an agitated state, having hallucinations and everything, we try to give them medication that will calm them down. And we watch them carefully so they can't hurt anybody, including themselves. Why?"

"But what if they're so bad even the hospital can't help them?"

She looked at me and smiled. She was the woman she'd been for a few minutes in the hospital the other night. "You're a very devious man, aren't you, Coldwell?"

"Not any more devious than anybody else in this God-fearing town."

She paused on the walk. A small group of cowboys drifted past on muddy horses. Three blocks away the player pianos were already starting to roll in the casino.

"You want me to get you into the Brooks House, don't you?"

"Everybody knows I'm a drunk."

"What if they catch you?"

"I don't know about you, Sonia, but I want to find Evelyn and make sure she's all right."

She thought a moment. "So do I." She glanced around,

as if somebody might be spying on us. "What've you got in mind?"

So I told her what I had in mind.

She smiled when I finished telling her my plan. "I didn't realize you were a thespian."

"Well, I'm not the only one who'll have to do a little bit of acting."

She laughed. "I was in the seventh grade spring play when I was a girl. And people said I was quite good."

"People being your mother and father."

"Yes," she said, "and my uncle and aunt."

We fell to walking again.

"I'll have to get Dr. Snead's approval to have you committed."

"Will that be tough?"

"Shouldn't be. He lets me make my own judgment about things like that. And since you don't have any kin in this part of the Territory, I won't need to get anybody to sign waivers."

"I know we're going to find her there."

She raised her eyes to mine. "You really love her, don't you, Mr. Coldwell?"

"I thought we were going to be Sonia and Mitch."

"You really love her, don't you, Mitch?"

"No fool like an old fool. I'm too old for her, I don't have a wooden nickel in the bank, and I doubt I've even got a job anymore after my run-in with Jeremiah Belden last night. But yes I do love her. How could I possibly deprive a beautiful young woman of a great catch like myself?"

"Yes, now that you put it that way, you are quite a catch, Mitch." Her Swedish accent was back. Certain words brought it out clearly. Quite a catch sounded like "vite a ketch."

"So you'll do it."

"I'll do it."

"How about eight o'clock tonight? In front of my boarding-house."

"I hope I don't start laughing," she said.

"I'll try not to overdo it."

We had reached the hospital. The sandstone was pretty in the early morning light.

In one of the second-story windows a young boy, no more than seven, looked longingly out at the day.

"You're a good friend to her," Sonia Eckstrom said as we reached the front door. "She's lucky to have you."

"Oh, yes," I said. "Real lucky."

"Tonight then, eight o'clock?"

"Eight o'clock," I said.

I watched her walk inside, big and purposeful, yet oddly graceful, too. I wondered what the hell she was all about, such contrasting moods of cool and compassion.

I walked on home, preparing myself for tonight's performance.

21

In the early afternoon, I walked down to the store and bought a bucket of beer and carried it, slopping over, back to Mrs. Byrnes's front porch, where I drank with a zeal that was easy for anybody to see.

Because I'd been limiting my drinking to a few hours in the evening, Mrs. Byrnes and the others who joined me on the porch kept looking at each other nervously.

Had I backslid?

Was I once again going to be the falling-down drunk who had embarrassed himself all over town?

Around four, just as the workingmen were appearing on the porch with their own buckets, I went up to my room and brought down a pint of whiskey. I sat there and drank and watched the horse-drawn trolley clang by. Then I drank some more.

Now they really started glancing at each other.

So I had backslid.

So I was once again the soak they both pitied and despised.

By five, the sinking sun painting the sky amber and aqua and gold, the shadows growing long and the song of playing children being silenced by mothers calling them in to dinner—by five, everybody but me and Mrs. Byrnes had drifted in to dinner. Her helper—she was very careful never to demean her by calling her "maid"—had fixed today's dinner, so Mrs. Byrnes was free to do what she wanted.

I looked at the moon. It was no longer full, but it still looked large in the sky. My breath was silver.

"Why don't you give me your whiskey?"

"It's cold, Mrs. Byrnes. Have you noticed that?"

"Yes, I've noticed that." Pause. "Mitch, did you hear what I said?"

"Yes, I heard."

"Why don't you do it, then?"

I didn't look at her. I just stared at the cold ragged mountains silhouetted against the glowing sky. The first stars were out.

"I need this right now, Mrs. Byrnes."

"You're already drunk."

"I don't feel drunk."

"Is it your son?"

"It's everything, Mrs. Byrnes. Everything."

"Evelyn Saunders?"

"A little, I suppose."

"She'll turn up. And she certainly won't be happy to see you if you're drunk."

"I'll have to take care of my own business, Mrs. Byrnes. There isn't any other way I can do it. But I appreciate your concern."

I lifted the pint. Had me some.

"At least come in and eat."

"In a little bit."

"You need food."

"I need a lot of things, Mrs. Byrnes." I'd intentionally started to slur my words. "Things" had become "shings."

"If you're having trouble walking, I can get one of the men to come out and get you."

"I appreciate that. But I'll be fine."

"It wouldn't be any trouble."

"I'll be in in a while."

She stared at me. "Please let me help you, Mitch. I just don't like to see you this way."

I made my movements rough, uncoordinated, the way you do when you're drunk and trying to act sober.

She stood up. I could hear her sniffling. Not the cold. Tears.

"You're just going to sit out here?"

"For the time being, Mrs. Byrnes."

She whispered something, but I couldn't hear what it was. Then she vanished into the lace curtains and the lamplight and the lilac scent of the parlor.

My first real performance came when I went inside and pretended to be climbing the stairs to my room.

I fell down, let myself roll back down a few stairs. And, just in case anybody had missed the physical part of my routine, I gave a little helpless shout.

They came running.

The two young bucks got me on my feet and carried me straight up to my room, where they put me flat on the bed and then held me down while Mrs. Byrnes held a lamp close to my face and looked for any damage.

"His eyes look all right, and nothing seems to be broken," she said.

"Dumb goddamned soak," said one of the bucks. "Pardon my French."

"He's a sad man," Mrs. Byrnes said. "You'd have to have children to understand."

She put the lamp back on the stand. Blew it out.

It was very dark. There were just the familiar shadows of the room and the pretty lilac scent of Mrs. Byrnes and the sweaty day-labor smell of the bucks.

I started snoring.

This seemed to please Mrs. Byrnes a great deal, the way you're pleased when a troubled child has finally settled into sleep for the night.

She closed the door behind her and gave the strapping bucks the order to tiptoe downstairs.

The second part of my performance started at 7:45, according to the grandfather clock chiming in the hallway.

I had fifteen minutes, and this was the part I had to make especially good.

I kept thinking of an old coot I'd known in the carnival several years back. He always got so bad with his nightmares, we had to feed him whiskey and literally tie him to his bed before he stopped screaming at the imaginary monsters persecuting him.

I got myself ready. I mussed my hair. I tore my shirt straight down the front. I undid my belt. And I took a fresh pint and doused my hair, face, arms, and legs with it.

They were in the parlor. Mrs. Byrnes was at the piano, playing something pretty, and the older men were reading their newspapers and yellowbacks. I had noticed as many as a dozen Nick Carters stacked on a small table just outside the bathroom we shared. Free for reading if you promised to bring them back.

I wasn't all that inventive an actor, I'm afraid.

I did my falling-down stunt again, only this time instead of falling down as I was going up the stairs, I fell down as I was going down the stairs.

They sounded as if they were kicking furniture out of the way trying to get through the parlor doors and see what the crash had been all about.

They found me sprawled at the bottom of the stairs, muttering deliriously.

I knew I'd better not try anything fancy, so I just kept saying over and over, "He's got a knife! He's got a knife!"

"What the hell's he talkin' about?" one of the old farts said, sounding peeved that I'd taken him from Nick Carter's derring-do.

"The crazies," said another old fart. "The whiskey crazies. That's what wrong with him."

"Oh Lord," Mrs. Byrnes said, "I'm afraid you're right."

They started to get me to my feet. That was when I went into my grand finale.

I let them stand me up, let them brush me off a little, let them cluck about what a bad boy I was and how they'd known all along it would come to this, and then I bolted.

I went right for the double front doors with the handsome stained glass windows.

I threw the doors open wide and screamed, "They're trying to kill me! These people are trying to kill me!"

All I could hope was that it was getting real close to eight o'clock because I sure couldn't keep this up much longer.

Being crazy was a lot harder work than I'd thought it was going to be.

They grabbed me again, but I wasn't going to let them keep me.

No, my turn on stage wasn't quite over yet.

I tore myself from their hands, stumbled forward across the porch, stumbled on down the front stoop, and then stumbled out into the middle of the lamp-lit street.

Where, of course, I gave them a crazy act that nobody in this entire neighborhood would ever forget.

"They're not really humans! They're monsters! And they're going to kill me!"

These were just a few of the things I shouted as I ran up and down the street.

People gawked out their windows and came out on their porches. Dogs barked and kiddies cried. Kitty cats hid under ottomans.

And still the madman ran up and down the street shouting. And waving his arms. And spraying spittle. And bugging out his eyes.

And still the people from his boardinghouse ran after him, cursing and shouting themselves, but never quite able to catch him.

And still the neighbors said to each other, "Whiskey crazy. Knew it would happen to that damned soak someday. Whiskey crazy."

And just where the hell was the good nurse Sonia Eckstrom during all these theatrics?

I figured I had about one more run up and down the street left in me when I heard someone with a definite Swedish accent say from the darkness, "Yah, that poor poor man. We'd better grab him before he hurts himself."

By now my boardinghouse crew had been joined by several other neighborhood men.

And they were only too eager to do Sonia Eckstrom's bidding.

By the time they slammed me to the ground, knelt on my ribs, hammerlocked my injured arm and held my head still with a handful of my hair, I figured I really was going to need a hospital.

But I kept it up.

Kept shouting about monsters and knives and phantoms and death.

And Sonia said, "Maybe one of you men had better slap him. I think that's what he needs."

The guy hit me so hard, he drew blood.

He needed to practice up on his medicinal slaps. Breaking somebody's jaw was not supposed to be part of the deal.

22

Fifteen minutes later I lay in the back of a wagon that smelled of hay and horseshit, the two younger men from the boardinghouse lashing my wrists and ankles with rope. Fifteen long minutes while Sonia ran off to Dr. Snead's house and got his permission to have me committed.

"He won't go nowhere now, ma'am," one of them said to Sonia Eckstrom.

"Thank you, gentlemen, I really appreciate this," she said.

One of the geezers held a torch nearby. The chill air smelled of kerosene. I looked up at the starry sky and tried, as usual, to make some sense of things, what the stars were and who'd put them there, and how it was that a man who loved his only son so much came to kill that son. But there was never any sense in pondering those questions because there are never any answers unless you're a quick slick preacher who can find a Bible passage for every trouble.

"You drive that rig all right?" somebody said.

To which Sonia Eckstrom took some offense. "I'm a modern woman. I can do what I need to do." Her voice was chillier than the air.

"Will we be able to visit him in the Brooks House?"

125

Mrs. Byrnes wanted to know, as Sonia walked around the front of the rig and climbed aboard.

"I won't know anything until I get there, Mrs. Byrnes. I'm sorry."

Mrs. Byrnes looked down at me in the bed of the wagon. I tried to look sorrowful. And crazed.

And I must have succeeded because she started sniffling. She put her long soft hand on my stubby hard one and stroked it. "He reminds me so much of my boy."

And, of course, I felt guilty, deceiving good-hearted Mrs. Byrnes this way. But at the moment I didn't have much choice.

"We'll be leaving now," Sonia said, sounding as if she was picking up the reins.

"You take good care of him."

"I'll do that, Mrs. Byrnes."

"You're an angel of mercy, Nurse Eckstrom."

"No call to say that, Mrs. Byrnes. I'm only doing my job."

"God damned soak," said one young man to the other, "shoulda known it would come to this."

" 'They ain't human. They're monsters, they're monsters!' " the second one mocked.

"You two boys should be ashamed of yourself," Mrs. Byrnes said. "And don't bother to ask me for extra pieces of pie tomorrow night, either."

"Aw, Mrs. Byrnes, we was just kiddin'," said the first one.

She might not be able to shame them with her scorn, but she sure could rattle them with her promises of extra pie withheld.

"Ernie's right, Mrs. Byrnes," said the second one. "Coldwell is just like an older brother to us. We're just as concerned about him as you are. Right, Ernie?"

"Absolutely right, Mrs. Byrnes. And by the way, what kind of pie did you say you'd be servin' tomorrow night?"

Apparently, Sonia did not hold the species of horses in high regard.

Not the way she drove them this night, anyway.

"How're you doing back there?" she shouted over her cracking whip as we plunged on across mercilessly rough stagecoach roads deeper into the dark night.

"Pretty good as long as I don't hit my head anymore. Because if I do, I'll probably have a concussion."

"Don't whine, Mr. Coldwell. It doesn't become you."

"Couldn't you slow down a little?"

"This is supposed to be an emergency. This is how you handle horses in an emergency. Now please be quiet and just lie there."

She didn't speak to me again until we were heading up a steep, piny hill that smelled of autumn smoke and sweet fallen pine needles.

She slowed down and said, "You'll have to do a little more performing when I get you up to the door."

"About like I was doing?"

"Maybe a little bit less. Especially the crying. You don't cry worth a darn, Mr. Coldwell."

"If I ever get the time, I'll practice more."

"And don't be sarcastic. In the condition you're in, you wouldn't have the wherewithal to be sarcastic. You understand?"

"Uh-huh."

"Just a little low moaning."

"All right. Low moaning."

"And maybe a little muttering."

"All right. A little muttering."

"And say that word 'monsters' sometimes. That's very good."

"Say 'monsters' sometimes. All right."

"And how about wetting your pants?"

"Wetting my pants?"

"It'd look very realistic. That's what drunken men do all the time."

"I don't know if I can. On purpose, I mean."

"Try."

So I tried. I looked up at the pretty moon and the pretty tops of the pines and the pretty pastel-colored clouds and I did my best.

I clenched my teeth and grunted and groaned and concentrated so hard I was giving myself a headache.

And I even sort of started talking to it down there. You know, kind of cajoling and threatening and begging it to let go with some pee.

But it's difficult. We're taught all our lives never to befoul our trousers this way, and we learn the lesson so well that it's hard to get around.

"How're you doing, Mr. Coldwell?"

"I thought you were going to call me Mitch."

"All right, Mitch, how're you doing?"

"Not very well."

"What's wrong?"

"What's wrong? Have you ever tried to pee in your knickers?"

"I'm a lady, Mitch. I'd never try anything like that."

"Well, it's not easy."

"Just close your eyes and imagine water."

"That won't work."

"Try it."

So I tried it. I imagined glasses of water . . . then little creeks . . . then streams then rivers then oceans then the kind of rainstorms that flooded out crops.

"Did that help?"

"No."

She sighed. "All right. Forget about it and just lie back. We're almost there."

The Brooks House had been built along the lines of a Bavarian castle, with two towers spearing up into the night sky and a half-dozen mullioned windows glowing with golden light. Unfortunately, the windows all had bars on them.

"Go into your act," Sonia Eckstrom whispered as the wagon clattered to a stop.

It wasn't as good as the first time. I was probably getting tired of it by now. And embarrassed. I moaned and cried and said "monsters" over and over, and then all of a sudden rough, competent hands were lifting me from the wagon and dropping me onto a canvas stretcher and carrying me through a narrow hallway that led up to a steep flight of stairs.

For the next few minutes I stared up the noses of two thickset men who showed absolutely no interest in my wailing and moaning.

In fact, just below the level of my dramaturgy, they were carrying on a conversation with Sonia.

"Alcohol?" one asked.

"Yes. Very bad. Starting to imagine things. They just couldn't handle him in town anymore, and we don't have those kind of facilities at the hospital."

"Fine. We'll get him in a room."

"Thank you."

After the third flight of stairs, I gave up the crying and went into trembling, legs and arms and head twitching violently.

"He's really bad," said one of the men.

"Yes," Sonia Eckstrom said. "Very bad."

I had the feeling she was referring to my performance.

The first place they put me was a small room with a lone

lamp sending eerie waves of mustardy light to the cold corners of the place.

I sat in a straight-backed chair. My wrists were handcuffed. My ankles were lashed together with twine.

The two men who'd done this had said, "We'll be right back. You just sit here and relax."

I just rolled my eyes and mumbled something, wanting to stay true to my character.

So I sat and waited. Where the hell was Sonia, anyway?

All I could figure out was that this was some kind of holding cell and that I would eventually be transferred someplace else.

The door opened.

I expected to see one of the guards come in.

Nobody came in for a time.

Then I saw his face. I recognized him right away, and even though I was supposed to be acting crazy, I couldn't help responding to him. Like most other people who had to look at him, I averted my eyes so I was looking just above and to the right of his shoulders.

"You know who I am, mister?"

"Yeah," I said, dropping my act for the moment. "Yeah, I do."

"You talk to me a little bit?"

I sighed. "I guess so."

"You don't really want to, do ya?"

"Not really."

"How come you're here?"

"I'd just as soon you leave, friend," I said.

"You hate me, huh?"

"I guess."

"They all hate me. In town, I mean. 'Cause of what I done and all."

His name was Ryan. He was a twenty-year-old farm boy. He got a town girl named Jennifer Aarons pregnant about two years ago. She went away and had the baby and came back, bringing the kid with her, going straight to Ryan and saying she expected him to marry her.

But Ryan didn't want to marry her. He was in love with another girl. So one night he set fire to the little creek shack where Jennifer and the baby lived.

But Ryan hadn't counted on an explosion, hadn't carefully considered the properties of kerosene.

The funny thing was, Jennifer and the baby got out fine. A little smoke in their lungs, but that was about all.

But Ryan . . .

Well, he was a monster, and no matter how long you looked at him, you couldn't ever quite get used to him.

There wasn't any face left, just suffering blue eyes and white teeth buried in skin as coarse and intricate as hand-tooled leather. . . .

His folks tried to handle him, but they couldn't. A local judge declined to sentence him to prison, saying God had given Ryan his very special punishment.

He went insane, was given to running up and down the street sobbing and wailing and grabbing people and shouting into their faces, "Look at me! Look at me!" and finally nobody in town could take it anymore so they stuck him out here in the nuthouse.

"You won't look at me, will you?"

"Why don't you get some rest, kid?"

"You know what I done and all, don't you?"

"Yeah, I guess I do."

"I'm really sorry I done it."

I sighed. "Kid, I can't help you. Don't you understand that? I can't fucking help you. Maybe I would if I could, but I've got problems of my own and—"

"Would you look at me just once?"

"Kid—"

"Just look at me. Right at me. Right in the face. Just for a little while. Please?"

"Shit, kid—"

"Please, mister, please . . ."

What else could I do?

I looked. It wasn't easy, not the way his face was.

"Just keep looking, mister. Just like that."

And then he started crying and I got all fucked inside, not knowing how to feel about any of this, wanting to kill him and yet wanting to hold him the way I would a little boy and—

"I appreciate it, mister."

He was crying now, hard sobs in his chest and throat, the tears coursing down the hand-tooled rivulets of his facial skin.

"I really do appreciate it, mister. I really do."

And then he was gone.

Suddenly there was no light. They had carried me into a room and put me on some kind of low single cot. They stripped away my bonds and then belted me down across chest and knees and wrists.

One of them had said, "Why don't you come with us and we'll get him signed in?"

"Very well," Sonia said.

The last light was them opening the door, the hallway glow framing the rectangle of door frame.

Then the door closed and there was no light at all, and the only sound, already eerie and distant, was the retreating slap of their footsteps on the stone stairs.

The leather straps made me feel more vulnerable than the ropes had. With the ropes, there'd at least been the illusion that I could somehow work them off me. But the straps . . . No way.

Then there was the darkness, a cold ocean that threatened

to drown me. I strained against the leather straps. I wanted to call out for Sonia, especially when I heard, somewhere on the floor above me, the unmistakable laughter of a crazy person, that high frantic sound that is half desperation and half lunacy.

But then I remembered Evelyn and forced myself back into control. I loved her. She was being held captive here. Spooky as this place was, I had to stay strong so I could help her.

And I was doing pretty well at staying strong, too, until I felt something crawling up my thigh in the darkness.

It was working its way up onto my chest with unhesitating confidence. I felt the way I had once when, back on the farm, I'd shoved my foot into my boot and a milk snake had started crawling up my pants leg.

But this wasn't a milk snake.

Not with its chittering. Not with its fecal smell. Not with its red hungry eyes.

No, this was a rat, and a big fearless one at that.

23

He must have been farsighted, the rat, I mean, because he stood on my chest squinting, as if trying to bring my face into focus.

I could smell him, I could feel his fat belly trembling, but I couldn't see much of him except his alien amber eyes.

I spent a few useless moments wrenching against my restraints, and then I just settled down and tried hard not to think about what those teeth of his could do to my face.

He took a few more quick tiny steps toward me. Still squinting. Making his high mincing noises again.

I pulled my face back as far away as I could get it and then I wondered, not being an expert on vermin, if he wouldn't maybe start with my throat.

Sweat stood heavy and cold on my forehead; my bowels tensed sickeningly.

Two more steps, he took.

I felt his whiskers brush against my throat.

The way he smelled, he must have spent the last half hour in an outhouse.

His noises got louder again, here in the cold, swimming darkness. An alien species for sure.

For a long moment, I couldn't help myself, I closed my eyes and tried to will him away. You know how you play those little nightmare games. Maybe when you open your eyes the thing will be gone . . .

But no. He was still there.

I tried to rock him off, turning as hard side to side as my straps would let me.

But he was a sure-footed bastard. He rode my chest like a bronc buster busting a mount at a rodeo.

In fact, when I got through pitching my body left and right, I discovered that the only thing I'd accomplished was to bring him closer to my throat.

I froze.

His hot slimy nose and mouth touched my Adam's apple while his whiskers teased the bottom of my jawline.

I wanted to scream, but I knew if they came in and found me like this, terrified but coherent, they'd know I'd been faking my whiskey crazies.

I rocked side to side again.

I tried to shrink inside myself so he couldn't quite reach me.

I started saying gibbering little prayers.

And I became aware, and not without some icy humor, of how close I was to wetting my pants.

More chittering.

The hot slimy nose seeming to burrow into my throat.

The madly twitching whiskers.

Little fucker. If I ever get my hands on you—

And then I felt the edges of his teeth start to tear my white vulnerable flesh and—

"Oh, my God!"

When Sonia opened the door, a rectangle of lantern glow angled across the room, showing her me strapped to the cot and the rat about to begin his feast.

She came fast across the room, taking the back of her hand and knocking the rat two feet into the air. It finally slammed hard against the wall.

"Why didn't you call for somebody?" she said.

I explained as best I could.

"I didn't think of that." She smiled. "You're a lot braver than I would have been."

She leaned down and put her hand to my forehead and pressed the sweat away with her palm.

"You're shivering."

"It's called cowardice."

"I'll find a blanket."

She went out the door to reappear half a minute later with a red blanket.

She put it over me, daubed at my forehead again.

She leaned in, spoke in whispers.

"We've had some good luck."

"Oh?"

"Dr. Greaves, who runs this place, isn't here tonight. His brother in Jasper County has a bad case of the gout so he's over there. That means nobody will be in to check you out tonight. One of the guards will peek in every once in a while, but that still should give you some time to look around and find Evelyn."

I nodded.

From the folds of her dress she took a .45.

"Here. It's loaded."

"Thanks."

She leaned over and kissed me chastely on the forehead.

"I didn't think proper Swedish women did things like that."

"Who said I'm proper?"

"Everybody in town."

"Maybe they're not as smart as you think."

I smiled. Even in the shadows here, even speaking in whispers, I could see that this kind of banter inhibited her. But she went on with it to show me that she was a human being, after all.

"You're all right, Eckstrom."

"Did I just pass a test or something?"

"No. But here you had me thinking you were this ice princess, when you're actually a very warm, decent woman."

"Well, I guess we're both surprised, then."

"Oh?"

"Here you had me thinking you were this hopeless soak who was the town joke."

"Sounds like a couple of nice people. An ice princess and a soak."

She pulled the covers over me. Then reached inside and unfastened my restraints.

"How does that feel?"

"How long do they leave people in these things, anyway?"

"Sometimes for days at a time," she said.

I rubbed my wrists for circulation. "If you weren't crazy before they put you in these, you sure would be afterward."

"Asylums aren't the nicest places. There are a lot of stories you hear that—"

She stopped speaking, *ssshed* me.

The hall. Footsteps.

A silhouette peeked in. "How is everything Nurse Eckstrom?"

Male voice. One of the guards.

"He's resting now. Doing better. I gave him the medicine. He should sleep through the night," Sonia said.

"I'll check him in a couple hours."

"Thank you for all your help."

"Nice to see you again, Nurse Eckstrom. Just let me know when you're ready to leave. I'll let you out."

Footsteps again, this time leading away.

"I'd better get back to town now," Sonia said.

"This place is pretty spooky."

"Just keep your gun ready."

"You're a nice woman, you know that? Even if you try to pretend otherwise sometimes."

"You're just talking so I have to stay here with you. You're afraid to be alone."

I laughed. "You're right. This place really scares me. Have you heard the laughter?"

"Yes, I have. Wait till you hear the screams over on the other side."

"The screams?" I said.

"Yes. I heard them earlier tonight. As I said, you hear a lot of stories about asylums."

"Any of them true?"

"I suppose."

She leaned down and tucked me in. "Take care of yourself, Mitch."

"Don't worry about that."

She looked at me a long moment, turned and left.

She closed the door behind her.

The cold currents of darkness had taken me down again. There was just the gloom and the chill and the faint echoes, above and below, of mad laughter.

24

I left my boots off. Less noise that way. I crept out the door of my room and down a long hall of six doors, three to a side. The only light came from a sconce on the stone wall. It guttered, casting long and ominous shadows.

I smelled stale food, sweat, feces, and faintly, cigarette smoke. I put my ear to each of the six doors, but heard nothing especially interesting, just the groans and sighs of people sleeping.

Mr. Blackemore had said that I'd find Evelyn on the third floor. This was the second.

Stairs wound upward so tightly that I got slightly dizzy going up them.

I heard the people before I saw them. All I could think of was a monkey cage in a zoo. How the animals called out to each other in various ways—curses and complaints, love calls and laughter.

That's what these people were doing, but they were human, so their bright, quick noises carried with them a burden of sorrow—because human beings, sane ones at any rate, were not supposed to sound like this.

The stone wall was cold as I pressed myself to it on the way up.

At the top of the stairs I took in a deep breath and started to ease myself around the edge of the wall.

There was a good chance a guard would be sitting there, carbine sitting across his lap, watching for me or anyone else who wasn't supposed to be there.

There was no guard.

As they started to see me, one by one, new bright noises quickened in their throats.

A novelty, a human toy, had been presented to them, and they responded like startled and excited children.

All I could think of was the zoo.

The third floor was one long, wide room with mullioned windows exposed by guttering candles, a dark and filthy room that smelled like a latrine and looked like the pens outside a slaughterhouse.

The floor was divided up to house four large cages filled with people in rags and tatters who were chained to the insides of their cages. They stared at me from their madness and their illness and their grief and their fear and their sadness, grateful for the respite I gave them. They had puked and shat and pissed and bled in these cages, and nobody official had been in any hurry to clean it up.

A note of glee swelled among them as those in back pushed their way to the nearest corner of their cages so they could see me better.

Their chains clanked; their fingers entwined with the bars of their cages. They clung to the bars tightly, as if soon they would be tearing them down.

"He's cute!" one of the women said.

"I'll bet he could get us out of here if he wanted to!" said a shrunken little man who appeared to be a bald dwarf.

"Ask him if he's got any whiskey!" a stout man said.

I went to the nearest cage, holding my breath because of the odors, my eyes glimpsing open sores and even what appeared to be broken bones.

I went to a sweet-faced middle-aged woman whose dark grave eyes seemed at least a little bit sane.

"I'm looking for a woman," I said.

Several of the men giggled and tittered. "A woman, he wants. We should give him old Maude."

"She died last week, don't you remember?" somebody else said.

"Give her to him anyway!" the first man said, laughing.

"There's a woman here," I said. And then I described Evelyn to her.

The woman listened as I spoke. She did not seem the least bit rattled by all the commotion around her. Her grave eyes held me fast.

Her calm seemed to affect the others. One by one they were silenced themselves, waiting for her to speak.

"Do you love this woman?"

"I guess I do," I told her.

"Does she know you love her?"

"I think so."

"You came to take her away from here?"

"Yes."

"Is she a good woman?"

"A very good woman."

"My husband called me a whore. And then put a hot poker up me."

She dropped her hand, to touch herself low on the groin. I didn't want to think about what she'd just said.

"I'm sure you're not a whore."

She started crying. Nothing dramatic. Just tears in her voice, tears on her cheeks. "He shouldn't have put that poker up me. I only went with Lem that one time to the creek."

I reached through the bars and touched her face.

"You're not a whore. You're a very good woman."

"He shouldn't have used that poker on me."

"No, he shouldn't."

I left my hand here, feeling her warm tears and the soft tremor that went through her as she recalled what her husband had done.

"You really don't think I'm a whore?"

"No, I don't."

She took my large hand in her two small, rough hands and kissed it.

"I hope you get your woman out of here."

"Will you tell me where she is?" I said softly.

She turned slightly and nodded to another set of stairs running along the back wall. "Up there. There's a room."

"Thank you."

They started in again, louder this time, their strange, convoluted, incomprehensible chatter, human monkeys in a human zoo.

They called me names, asked me for favors, dared me to do certain things, pleaded with me to help them escape.

There were whistles and catcalls and the crazed laughter again, eerie and sad by turns, as if I were looking at another species I could not understand but only pity.

And then, above the din, the woman just now letting go of my hand, I heard the unmistakable crack of a leather whip.

The sound cut through everything, just as the tip of its lash would cut through flesh, and the faces that had been grin-split only moments ago, now were screwed up tight in dread and fear.

They moved as one, from the front of the cages to the back, shuffling and hunching down in defensive crouches, all their eyes on the top of the stairs.

The whip cracked again. Footsteps echoed off the narrow stairway walls. He appeared, within moments, on the edge of the last step.

He was a skinny hayseed bastard. I could have pushed

his face in with one hand. But he had some kind of official khaki uniform, and he had some kind of official badge, and he had his very official bullwhip. So the fact that he was a runty, laughable little prick didn't matter.

To the people in the cages, he was obviously the darkest of dark gods, a man not of mercy, but of guile and cruelty. He alone determined their fate, and he obviously relished his punky little powers.

By this time I'd moved across the floor to crouch in the shadows of the stairs that ran to the top floor.

He didn't see me. He was too busy putting on a bad cornball show with his whip. He was bad with it, imprecise, awkward, clumsy—the worst carny in the worst show in the worst season could have done better with that whip—but he mesmerized the cage people with the promise of horrors to come.

They watched rapt and paralyzed as his whip lashed closer and closer to the cage, driving them deeper back, into even more of a timorous little clutch of people.

"You know what time it is?" he said. "Huh?"

"Yes, Mr. Gwyn, we know what time it is."

They said this in unison, like a kindergarten class proud of itself and preening.

"You were supposed to be asleep an hour ago. Is that right?"

"Yes, Mr. Gwyn."

The chorus again.

Then fearful silence as he started some cornball pacing up and down the front of the cages, cracking his whip every few feet.

"Who did I put in charge tonight?"

This time, silence.

"Does anybody remember who I put in charge tonight?"

"You put Tony in charge," somebody from the back said.

"Tony, Tony," they said in unison.

"Is that right, Tony?"

He was this big blubbery guy, fat and cowardly and sad as shit, with the eyes of a whipped dog.

"You know what happens now, Tony?"

"Yessir, Mr. Gwyn."

"I put you in charge tonight."

"Yessir, Mr. Gwyn."

"And you let me down."

"Yessir, Mr. Gwyn."

"Come on out of there."

"I don't want to, Mr. Gwyn."

Gwyn looked at the others. Grinned. "You know what happens if Tony isn't out of there in one minute?"

The unison again. "Yes, Mr. Gwyn."

"You all get whipped. One by one."

Tony said, "We was only makin' noise 'cause of that fella."

"Fella? What fella? What the hell you talkin' about, 'fella'?"

Tony pointed to the narrow staircase leading up the wall to the final floor.

At first Tony, when he turned his head toward me, didn't see me. The only light in the big room was a few small torches in sconces. The light was brown and murky. And I had the shadows to hide me.

But then, puzzled, he turned around completely and walked toward me.

"Is there a fella over there?"

True to his rube roots, he wasn't at all afraid of me. He was eager to get me caught up in the lash of his bullwhip. He was god to the poor crazy bastards filling the cages; so by now, Gwyn obviously figured he was god to everybody else, too.

I didn't wait for him to come over to me.

I came up out of the shadows, my gun pointed directly at his head.

"I want your whip."

"Fuck you talkin' about, mister?"

"Just what I said, shitkicker. I want your whip."

"You real tough with your arm in a sling, are you?"

"Tough enough to kill some cracker asshole like you with one arm."

He looked at my Colt. Smirked. "You shoot that thing off in here, mister, you'll have every fuckin' guard in the place on you."

"Yeah, but you'll be dead."

That one, he was smart enough to think over.

"How about it, hayseed, do I get your whip or do I drop you right here?"

"Fucker."

"The whip."

"Fuckin' fucker."

"There's a catchy one." I walked closer, half eager to empty my gun in his dumb, ugly bullyboy face.

For practice I got him on the temple with the handle of my Colt.

He was an obedient boy, this shitkicker, he fell straight down without hesitating to the floor. Blood was already running from his head down his cheek.

He was sprawled out on his back now, trying desperately to get up. I went over and stepped on his chest, grinding my heel into his breastbone. It was pure pleasure watching the bullyboy in so much pain.

But he wasn't done yet. Oh, no.

I stuffed my Colt into my belt then got my good fingers on the handle of the whip. I wouldn't be any more amateurish at it than he was.

I stepped back so I could get some good lashes at him.

"This hayseed here whip you, does he?" I said to all the people lined up, fascinated, inside their cages.

"Uh-huh."

"Damn betcha he does."

"Sonofabitch. He whupped Ida till she died."

"He did, huh?" I said.

Before I started, I said to the hayseed, "You're going to get thirty lashes, shitkicker, you understand me?"

"Hey, listen, fuck, I mean—"

He was too scared to make any sense.

"Now as long as you don't scream out, the lashes are all you're going to get. Same thing you do to these poor people every night. You understand me?"

He tried to speak but he was still too scared.

"Now if you scream out, you're really going to have it bad, because every time you scream, I'm going to come over there and kick you in the mouth. You get me?"

"Hey, shit, listen, really I—"

"Just nod yes or no. Do you understand what I just said?"

He obviously wanted to say something else.

"Now, do you understand our little game here? Thirty lashes if you don't scream out. But I kick you every time you do. *Comprende*, cocksucker?"

He nodded, slowly and sadly, knowing what was coming.

The people in the cages were excited, quietly clapping their hands together, jumping up and down like excited children.

"Shit," he said.

I got him five good lashes across the chest, and then when he rolled over, clamping his trembling hand over his mouth, I gave him five bloody fast ones on his back, ripping hell out of his shirt and lacerating his flesh.

Five more lashes, one of them snaking around his throat, choking him momentarily.

"If I ever find out that you whipped any of these people again, I'm coming back to get you. All right?"

He nodded again. He was crying. His face ran with tears and snot.

I lashed him five more times across the chest. He rolled left and right but he couldn't get away.

On the last lash, he screamed.

I smiled. He was every bully who'd ever pushed me around or insulted me or humiliated me. Just some no-brain bullyboy who took great pleasure in other people's pain.

"You screamed," I said.

"Not loud."

"That wasn't our agreement. Our agreement didn't have anything to do with loud. You know that."

"Aw, shit, mister, please—"

I got him right in the mouth. Beneath the toe of my boot I could feel some of his teeth go. He vomited up thick dark blood, staining his shirt and the floor.

"He's got more comin', don't he?" the dwarf in the cage said.

I shook my head, hurled the bullwhip in the corner.

"I don't want to be like him. And that's just what I'm doing."

"Aw, just a couple more?" the dwarf said.

"Sorry."

"You should ought to see what he does to us'n every night."

"I know. But he won't be doing it anymore. I'm going to tell the city council about it."

But by now I wasn't paying any attention. I was digging through a small wooden box of tools in the far corner. I found just what I wanted. Enough rope to tie up the hayseed. I ripped his shirt up to use as a gag.

By the time I started up the stairs to the next floor, Gwyn had fallen into a deep, loud sleep.

"You gonna get your woman, mister?" asked the woman whose husband had used the poker on her.

At the moment she looked like a moony young woman. "I wish I was your woman, mister. I wish you was takin' me away with you."

I smiled sadly, wishing there was something I could do for her, knowing that there wasn't.

In this man's west, a husband could get a wife locked up for all sorts of reasons, not the least of which was adultery. Happened all the time.

And every court in the land sided with the prerogative of the husband to put her in an asylum if she betrayed him.

How could anybody betray a sweet loving husband like himself, never mind that he beat the shit out of her every couple of nights, and beat up the kids, too, if they dared complain about how their mother was being treated?

A nice swell guy like that.

Bitch belonged in a loony bin.

I went upstairs to get Evelyn.

25

I assumed that the door, the small mahogany door at the top of the stairs, would be locked. I had my gun drawn, my foot ready to kick in the wood if necessary, and I was working up some real anger.

I turned the knob to the left. The door opened. No derring-do on my part was required. The way the bullyboy had left me feeling, I was almost disappointed.

Except for starry sky in a westward-facing window, there was no light in the small apartment I'd just walked into.

Several pieces of good furniture, including a couch and two chairs, filled the room. Mexican art hung on the wall.

I closed the door. There was only starlight now. The sounds from the cages below were faint. This apartment had been built to shut out sound.

Three doors opened into other rooms. If she was up here, where was she?

I stood very still, listening.

Mostly, I heard my own breathing.

I went to the first door, listened. No sound at all.

I tried the second. The same. Utter silence.

The third, however, held promise.

I wasn't sure what I was hearing but I heard something, some faint noise.

I tried the knob. Locked.

Why would this be locked and the apartment door not be?

I went over to a table sitting between the two chairs, felt around on the surface. Nothing.

I went over to the mullioned window, felt along the rough, cool edge. Nothing.

I went over to the front door, stood up on tiptoes and felt along the frame on top.

It was right there waiting for me, a nice long silver key.

I took it over to the third door and inserted it.

Would this be the right one?

Would Evelyn be on the other side of the door?

I turned the key. The door opened.

I stood on the threshold, looking at the gently sleeping form of Evelyn Saunders on a double bed. The faint noise I'd heard had been the bedsprings as Evelyn shifted around in her sleep.

I went quietly across the room, leaned down and touched her shoulder.

She didn't come awake right away, and when she did, she gave a little gasp and glanced disoriented and scared around the shadowy room. There was a small rectangle of window above her bed, but only the starry night filled it.

"Mitch—how did you get in here?"

"No time to talk now. I'll explain it all later."

"But—"

"I came to get you."

Her eyes were starting to fill her face now. She looked baffled and scared. She was starting to awaken and to compose herself a little. A ceramic pitcher stood on her night table. She eased her legs off the bed, sat forward, poured herself some water.

"Want some?"

"No, thanks," I said. "I'm just glad to see you alive."

"Oh, Mitch."

She stood up, pressed some of the wrinkles from her dress with her hand. "I'll bet I look pretty bad."

"You look beautiful."

"This isn't how a girl likes to be seen."

"We'd better hurry, Evelyn. We'll get into town and get some help."

I took her in my arms, wanting to say a lot of things, but knowing this wasn't the time. I closed my eyes and felt the shape of her small head beneath my big hand. I held her with real reverence, and took in the sweet warm smell of her sleepiness, the way a kitten smells sweet just after sleep.

She hugged me back, mumbling my name several times and then easing away from me.

She was at the night table again, pouring water from the pitcher into a basin. When she got an inch or so in there, she set the pitcher down and put her hands in the water.

She started daubing her face with the water, patting it on her eyes and cheeks especially.

"C'mon," I said. I smiled. "I'm only going to feel lucky so long. Getting out of here isn't going to be easy."

I took her hand and tugged her out of the room and into the front of the apartment.

"Just stay right behind me and don't say anything. One way or the other, I'm going to get us to that front door and we're getting out of here. All right?"

"Mitch—" she said.

"Let's go," I said.

And that was when I heard him, a big man coming up behind me. I tried to twist away from the rifle butt he was bringing down on my head, but—

26

"I'll be all right. I need to tell him what's going on here." Female voice.

"He may get mad. After being knocked out and all." Male voice.

"It's my fault and I'll tell him that. I should have stopped you before—"

Silence.

"He sounds like he's coming to. Please leave me alone with him. I'll be fine. I really will."

"If you're sure." Male voice.

I heard all this as I swam my way up through fathoms of darkness to full light and full sound. The woman speaking was Evelyn, of course. I had no idea who the man was.

I had apparently fallen on my slinged arm, because it was hurting now as it had right after the wound.

I was on a bed, the springs squeaking as I sat up.

A door closed softly.

"Oh, poor Mitch. I'm so sorry this had to happen to you."

Dizziness. I stopped halfway up. Rested my head on my knee.

Evelyn's cool hand touched my cheek and ear. "Poor Mitch. I shouldn't have let him hit you. I tried to explain to him but— There just wasn't time. He moved before I could— Oh, Mitch, I'm so sorry. He was just trying to protect me. He thought you were—"

I got one eye open. In the small room the color of clean sand, a lamp with a flowered vase sat on a battered bureau, flame dancing beneath its red and blue and green buds. A cheap painting of a sad and emaciated Christ looked down on us from the east wall. The bed I was in had no sheets or covers.

"You've got me real confused, Evelyn. I don't know what's going on."

"Let me get you some water, then I'll explain."

"I'd appreciate it."

She went to a small table to the right of the bureau, poured splashing water into a glass and then came back to me.

She opened my good hand and put the glass in it. "Drink, Mitch. You need it."

I drank, nearly finishing it all off in two long, wet gulps.

She took the glass back to the table, poured more for me, and came back.

As I started drinking again, she said, "Do you remember the night Steve was killed?"

"Sure."

"And his father came up to me and blamed me."

I nodded. Nodding hurt.

"Well, knowing his father as I do, I knew I would probably have an 'accident' very soon. He tries not to have his enemies shot outright. That would be bad for appearances in the community. But his enemies do have 'accidents' at an alarming rate. And most people in town accept them as that. If they hear otherwise, they don't believe it. Or, they don't want to believe it because Belden is so generous with his money."

"You were afraid he'd have you killed?"

She touched my arm. In the lamp glow she looked young and devastatingly pretty. I ached to hold her, kiss her. At that moment I didn't give a damn what her story was, how she'd come to be here or what she was doing here, I just wanted to hold her and tell her how much I loved her.

But she wanted to tell me everything. "Before he died, Steve gave me four thousand dollars to keep. I'm not sure, but I think he managed to take it when he was working at his father's casino. Anyway, I decided to use that money to help get me out of town. So I paid the marshal and Karl Leifer and my father to help me with my story."

"You had to pay your own father?" She didn't seem to have any clue that the bastard was actually her stepfather. I wasn't going to tell her, either.

She shrugged. "I don't have any illusions about my father. I knew that Jeremiah Belden would come looking for me. He'd do what he always does—pay people so much money that they get their heads turned and then they betray their own kin. I figured the marshal and Leifer could probably hold out against Belden, but I didn't think my father could. So I gave him extra money. The other two got a thousand apiece. My father got two thousand."

She stood up, walked over to the window, looked out at the moonlit sky.

"You should see this, Mitch. There's a hawk flying across the moon just now. It's so beautiful."

I let her walk around a little more. Go back to talking when she was ready.

"So, anyway, Mitch, I came up with this story about me getting on the early train and Leifer seeing me, and my father not knowing where I'd gone. So it sounded as if I'd left town for good. And nobody knew where. Especially Jeremiah Belden."

She came over and sat next to me on the edge of the bed. She took my good hand and held it gently.

"I just needed a few days to think things over, make plans for where I wanted to go. I have a friend who's a nurse here. It was her idea that she could hide me out for a little while. Belden would never think to look in an asylum."

I remembered a few nights ago, seeing a very friendly Saunders drinking with a very friendly Belden at the casino bar. I decided against telling her. No sense making her worry any more than she was already.

She sighed. "But now I'm going. I had a worker from here ride to Ridgeton and send a telegraph for me—you know, if I'd sent it from Belden City, Jeremiah would have known about it in five minutes—and anyway, today I heard back. There's a friend of mine I went to nursing school with in Rochester, Minnesota. She's going to let me live with her for a while. She even thinks she can get me a job at the hospital where she works."

I tried to look happy for her, but I couldn't. Not quite. She was going away and there was a better than fair chance that I'd never see her again.

"I'm sorry I wasn't able to tell you what's really been going on until now." She shook her head. "The guards tonight— They were told to take care of anybody who they didn't know. I wasn't sure I was going to tell you all this, so when I saw them I froze and—"

I leaned forward and kissed her tenderly on the mouth.

"You're not mad?" she said afterward.

"No. Just impressed."

"Impressed?"

"With you and the way you were able to outsmart Jeremiah Belden."

"Now I'm just anxious to get out of here. Leave all the bad memories behind."

I could hardly speak. "I'm going to miss you. But I guess you know that."

"You've been so darned nice to me, Mitch. Maybe someday . . ."

Neither of us said anything for a time. Her words, "Maybe someday . . ." lingered on the air. A mere formality to her—she didn't want to hurt my feelings—and false hope for me. I'd cling to her "Maybe someday" for a long, long time after she was gone.

Finally I said, "When are you leaving?"

"Just before dawn."

"That's just a few hours."

She kissed me again. "I really am going to miss you, Mitch. I really am." She took my shoulders. Leaned me back.

"You need some rest. You really look beat."

"I'll be fine. I don't want to waste our last few hours—"

She touched a finger to my lips. "Just a little nap is all. I have to finish packing. We'll meet the train up the line, away from Belden City. I'll come in and see you before I go."

She pressed me farther back against two naked pillows.

"You really do need some rest, Mitch." She smiled. "Especially after that knock on the head." She paused. "You're a very fine man, Mitch Coldwell. You really are. Your wife was crazy to leave you."

"Oh, yes, I'm a real prize. And believe me, she had plenty of reasons to leave me. Plenty."

"See? That's how nice you really are. Defending your wife even after she walked out on you."

I hadn't thought of my ex-wife in a while. Now I saw her face in the days following our son's funeral, saw the sorrow and confusion and panic. And I'd helped put it there. No, there was no way I'd ever blame her for doing what she'd done. She'd just been trying to survive the best way she knew how. Sometimes that's all a person can do.

"I'll write you once a week," she said, kissing me again.

"I wish I could say the same. I'm not much of a letter writer."

"You will be, you'll see." The kid in her smiled at me. "You'll be so inspired by my letters, you'll start writing your own."

"You promise?"

"I promise."

I drew her to me and kissed her a final time. "Tell me again how we're going to meet up somewhere down the line."

"Oh, we are."

"You really think so?"

She crossed her heart. "I really think so, Mitch."

She stood up. "Now I've really got to pack. I'll see you in a little while. For now, get some rest, all right?"

I nodded.

"More water?"

"No, thanks," I said.

She went over and turned the lamp down.

At the door she looked back and smiled again, but this time I saw a little sadness in her eyes.

I was vain enough to think that I'd put that sadness there, that she was just as sorry about us splitting up as I was.

She closed the door softly and vanished.

27

There is the sleep of exhaustion, and the sleep of illness. I slept them both, much sooner and harder than I'd imagined I would.

There were dreams, disturbing but shapeless dreams, muted screams and the half-glimpsed faces of people without eyes or mouths, people chasing me down long glowing tunnels, and then—

Then I was awake.

At first I had no sure idea where I was. Against the window dawn was just starting to paint the sky a pearly lavender.

Some kind of noise had awakened me, but what—

Then I heard it.

Voices arguing outside my door.

At first they sounded as if they were part of my nightmare, angry, insistent, but curiously soft voices.

I closed my eyes. Listened. No, they weren't imaginary, the voices. They were right outside my room.

Getting up was not easy. My head pounded, the pain in my wounded arm ran from shoulder to fingertips, and my knees were wobbly. I was sweaty and chilled and achy. Too much had happened to me in my weakened condition.

But I found my Colt, tried for a third time to stand on my feet, and then walked unsteadily toward the door.

I opened it inward with a single jerk, and there they stood.

Evelyn and her father.

Both of them turned to look at me, startled.

"You shouldn't be up so soon," Evelyn said, the nurse in her taking over again.

"What's he doing here?" I said.

"You got no call to mess in any of my family business," Saunders said. As usual, his clothes looked dirty and wrinkled. His eyes held rheumy indignation, as if I were somehow the source of all his bad luck. "Some soak like you."

"Father!" she said.

I was tempted to tell her that he wasn't really her father, but that would hurt her far more than it would hurt him. He wouldn't give a damn either way.

"What's he doing here?" I said again.

"He went and talked to Sonia and told her how he was going crazy not knowing were I was and— Well, she felt sorry for him and told him what you'd found out." She looked at him and smiled. "I know you don't care for him, Mitch. But I am glad to see him."

"Where's Jeremiah?" I said to Saunders.

I was starting to understand what was going on here, even if Evelyn wasn't.

"Jeremiah?" she said.

But you could see it in the way his shoulders suddenly slumped, in the way his eyes went hangdog and guilty.

He had sold her out.

"Where is he?" I said to Saunders.

"He wouldn't have brought Jeremiah," she said. "He wouldn't betray me that way."

"Sure he would," I said. I glared at him. "Tell her, Saunders. Tell her the truth for once."

He touched Evelyn's arm with a grubby hand. "He said he just wants to talk to you, Evelyn. He promised me he wouldn't hurt you."

She was staring at him in grief and disbelief. "You brought Belden with you—"

"Honey, Evelyn, listen. He gave me his sworn word he wouldn't hurt you. He—"

By the time I heard them, it was too late to do anything much except watch them come at us.

Four of them, all with shotguns, two coming down the corridor from the west, two coming down the corridor from the east.

One of them was Jeremiah Belden. The others were three of his familiar thugs.

"You remember what you promised me," Saunders said as Belden drew near. "You gave me your word—"

"Can it, Saunders," Belden said, imposing as ever. "You got your money. You don't have any say from now on."

Saunders started to say something to Evelyn, but one of the thugs grabbed him from behind by both biceps and dragged him away.

"Evelyn, I'm sorry," he called over his shoulder as they took him away. "I'm sorry."

I sensed that he really was sorry, surprising both me and himself probably. But I didn't care. Not now. He'd handed Evelyn over to the man who wanted to kill her. No amount of sorry was ever going to make up for that.

Belden said, "You're coming with me, Evelyn. I've got a wagon downstairs."

He nodded to the room where I'd been sleeping. "You go sleep it off, Coldwell."

"Don't go," I said to her.

Belden hit me without any warning, hit me hard enough to slam the back of my head against the door frame, hit me ard enough to cost me consciousness for a few moments while I was still on my feet.

One of the toughs stepped up then and drove a fist deep into my belly. Then his knee came up to meet my jaw as I started to fall forward.

I started to sink, fast and sure.

There was only sound now, Evelyn crying out, jingle of spur, scrape of shoe leather as she was dragged down the corridor and down the stairs to Belden's wagon.

Only darkness now, darkness . . .

"You all right?"

When I came to, I found him peering down at me. Even in the shadows, his face made me queasy, the coarsened, leathery look of the skin.

"Where'd they go?"

"I 'preciate you lookin' at me straight on and all."

So what could I do? I had to keep looking at him. Straight on and all.

Maybe it was the pleading in his eyes that people looked away from. Maybe it wasn't the skin at all. Just the silent cry of the gaze.

I said again, "Where'd they go?"

"Took her downstairs, they did. Got a wagon waiting for her, they do."

I started to struggle up from the doorway. He helped me. You tended to forget he was a strong young man despite the burns.

"Did they leave yet?"

"Just pulling out, I think."

I looked down the corridor to the staircase. I was too weak to make it.

In the momentary silence I heard it, a heavy wagon just now starting to pull away, chink of traces, rumble of wide tired metal wheels. Only the latest model for a man like Jeremiah Belden.

"You that trick shooter, ain't you?" he said.

"Yes, why?"

"Seen you once when they brung us into town for an afternoon. You shoot real good. I know a place right down the hall where you might get a shot at them."

I didn't need any more elaboration. I held onto the sleeve of his shirt as he hurried me down to the end of the corridor, where we turned into a darkened room.

"Old Simmy's got the only window that opens a'tall."

Simmy, I took it, was the ancient man just now sitting up in his bed, looking more curious and angry than scared.

"Hey, you ugly bastard, what the hell you doin' in my room?"

"Fella here needs to use your window."

"Yer always runnin' around here upsettin' people," Simmy said, his bald head bobbing about in the shadows.

Then, as if to convince me that he really was an old fellow, with all the appropriate plumbing problems, he practiced the ancient art of flatulence with a ferocity that was stunning.

"Damn beans they serve here, anyhow," he said.

But by now I wasn't listening. I was crouching down in front of a window that would only open two inches.

"They're afraid we'll jump, that's why it only opens this far." The kid smiled. "But the way Simmy here stinks up a room, they've got to give it at least a little ventilation."

Two floors below me the wagon was just starting to pull down the long road winding back to town.

I had at most a few seconds before they would be out of pistol range.

"Good thing this fella's a sharpshooter. Wouldn't be able to hit 'em otherwise."

"Please be quiet," I said, trying to sight, getting ready to fire.

I had maybe six, seven seconds from my estimation.

"Told ya you talk too much," Simmy said, and then let go with another example of his prowess.

It was a big farm wagon, the three thugs sitting down in back, Belden and Evelyn up front.

I decided to take the thugs out first. The trouble was, did I trust myself to hit them and not hit Evelyn? Gripping the gun, trying to become familiar with it in the few seconds I had, I squeezed off—one—two—three—

The horses cried and bucked. The three thugs slumped forward. One I got in the face, one I got in the side of the head, one I got in the chest.

That was when Jeremiah Belden, grabbing a carbine from the seat, turned back, horrified, to see what had happened, and that's when I put two bullets right into his brain.

He was dead before his body knew he was dead, jerking this way and that, reaching forth an empty hand to grab only emptiness, falling sideways from the wagon seat to the floorboards beneath it.

"Sonofabitch!" the kid cried. "Sonofabitch!"

"Did he get 'em?" Simmy wondered from his bed.

"Did he get 'em? Told you he was a sharpshooter, didn't I?"

I left them to their argument, trying to get downstairs to Evelyn as quickly as possible.

28

The sobbing and the screaming and the cries for help were oppressive as I walked down the three flights of stairs to the front door.

The asylum inmates had been awakened to the sounds of gunfire and people dying. Not exactly the kind of reassurance that somebody in their predicament needed.

I didn't see any of the guards. They were probably trying to corral people back to their rooms. I wondered what the people in the cages made of all this.

Dawn was ripe now, the sun starting to beam full and golden over the horizon. The air was tangy and fresh with pine.

Evelyn stood dazed several yards down from where the wagon had stopped, the horses standing quiet now in their traces.

One of the thugs sprawled half out of the wagon end, his chest shiny and wet with blood, his eyes staring dumbly up at the sky.

I walked past Evelyn to see the rest of it. In the wagon bed two corpses lay facedown, their hands clawed as if they had, right at the last, tried to scuttle away to safety. They smelled pretty bad. At least one of them had shit himself.

164

I went up front and pulled Jeremiah Belden to a sitting position.

He didn't look very important now, with half his face little more than a grotesque, bloody hole. I almost felt sorry for him. Almost. But then I thought of all the people whose lives he had controlled for so long. Some of my old anger came back.

The flies were busy already, busy around his wounds. As the day got hotter, there'd be more of them and they'd have themselves a picnic.

"He's dead?"

I nodded.

Evelyn's voice had sounded surer, less shocked than I would have guessed.

I walked back up to her.

"I suppose I didn't have to kill him. But I was in a hurry."

She looked directly at me. My breath caught a little. I was afraid of her. Anybody who's got that much power over you is sure to scare you.

"Is my father all right?"

I nodded. "He was downstairs drinking coffee when I saw him a minute ago."

She looked around. "It's so strange."

"What is?"

"Listen. To the birds. They sound so sweet. And it's going to be such a beautiful autumn day." She shuddered and nodded to the wagon. "For everybody but them."

"I didn't know how else to do it."

She reached up and touched her soft, cool hand to my face. "You did what you had to, Mitch. Nobody can blame you. I just meant that it's all so strange lately. Everything. My whole life."

"You won't have to go away now."

I put my good hand on hers where it pressed my cheek. She took it gently away.

"Oh, no, Mitch. I'm still going."

I felt as if somebody had just told me I had two hours to live. "But—"

She came closer. "Mitch, now I need to get out of Belden City more than ever. All these terrible memories."

"But I was hoping that we could—"

I stopped myself.

No sense in begging. She wasn't the kind of woman who made her mind up frivolously, which meant she wasn't the kind of woman who would change it frivolously, either.

She had determined that it would be better for her to leave Belden City. I wouldn't be able to change her mind.

"Somebody from the asylum here is going to give me a ride up the line to the depot." She touched my cheek again. "I'll say good-bye before I leave."

She did exactly what I wanted her to do and exactly what I didn't want her to do.

She kissed me on the lips, a tender and prolonged kiss, and I felt all sorts of things I didn't want to feel but I was glad I did.

"Mitch, I meant what I said. Maybe someday you and I will meet up again."

"And maybe not." I felt cold and alone and scared.

"Maybe not, Mitch. That's right. But we're both adults and we have to take the chances adults do." The quick bright smile again that died like a falling star in the night. "Now I need to go in." She pointed to a buggy just appearing around the corner. A plump old man in a dark suit and gray beard drove it. "I'm late already."

I was just about to suggest that I'd help her bring her things down when I heard, echoing up the road behind me, the sound of three horses coming fast.

"That's probably going to be the marshal," I said. "I'm sure he heard all the fireworks."

"Well, I'll leave that for you to handle. Now I need to go get ready."

She hurried away.

I stood there watching the lawman and two of his deputies coming around the bend, riding hard and straight for the asylum.

As soon as they got within sight of the place, the deputies pulled their carbines.

29

Marshal Shay spent fifteen minutes just walking around and around the wagon, examining the bodies, looking up at the window I'd done my shooting from, and swatting flies away from the dead human meat.

About the third time he looked up at the third floor window, he said, "Your sharpshooting came in handy. No regular gunny could ever have done that."

I shrugged. "I was trying to save her life."

He watched my face, then smirked. "You're sweet on her just like Steve was, huh?"

I felt my cheeks get hot. "I shot these men because I had reason to believe they were going to kill Evelyn."

He nodded. "I'm going to surprise you a little bit, son, and agree with you. Word I got from Jeremiah's boys was that he blamed her for everything and was going to take care of her any way he had to."

"You're not going to charge me?"

"Well, there's some legalities to handle with the judge and all, but no, I don't see any reason to charge you."

He put long hands to the small of his back, stretched, and yawned like a big comfortable animal.

"There's somebody here I want you to take care of for me," I said. I told him about our friend with the bullwhip.

"You hear a lot of stories about the asylum."

"This isn't a story. I saw him and I saw the whip."

He kept his eyes on me several moments after I quit speaking, then nodded. "All right, Coldwell, I'll see that he's fired."

The sunlight was golden now, and the early morning dew on the grass was silver, and the birds sang long and pretty to the waking day. Marshal Shay seemed to have the same appreciation for all this that I did.

"Last of the good fishing for a while," he said, walking around the wagon again. "Think I'll take a day off and go up on the lake."

When he got to Jeremiah Belden this time, he paused, lifted a wide lifeless hand, and looked at the imposing Masonic ring that rode the third finger.

"I'm a Mason, too," he said, eyeing the ring. He carefully set the hand back, turned to face me. "I don't suppose you'll believe this, Coldwell, but he wasn't nearly as bad as most men who run towns like this. He wasn't any angel, that's for sure, but he pretty much let civic business run on its own without interfering."

"Unless it got in his way."

He squinted at me. "Don't suppose I can blame you for not liking him, way he treated you and all. But then the way you were drinking for a while there ... Well, you weren't exactly a shining fine example of good, decent manhood, either."

"No," I said, "I guess that's about the only thing nobody's ever accused me of. Being a shining fine example of good, decent manhood."

He smiled. "I'm surprised you were able to remember all that. Those are my pa's words. Back in Kansas, he was a preacher."

His deputies had been inside talking to people. They came out now and stood by the wagon, fascinated by the look and smell of death. Though they talked to the marshal, they couldn't keep their eyes from the corpses.

"Inside they said that Coldwell here is telling the truth," the first deputy said.

"Jeremiah come in and took Evelyn out at gunpoint and forced her to get in the wagon," the second deputy said.

"Damn flies," said Marshal Shay, swatting a few more away.

"They said Coldwell didn't have no choice but to shoot," said the first deputy. Now he started swatting flies from the corpses, too.

"Tollmer," said the second one, nodding to the chunkier of the three dead thugs, then holding his nose in a jokey way, "he shit his pants, and woooee does he smell bad."

The first deputy laughed. "Yeah, I'd sure hate to sit next to him at dinner tonight."

The marshal led me back toward the asylum. "I'd better be getting back to town, Coldwell. There's a council meeting over to Ivy's restaurant at nine sharp, and they'll want to hear all about Jeremiah and everything."

He mounted his horse. His two deputies came over and did the same.

"You want me to ask the council if they're still interested in having you run the Western Museum? It'd bring in a nice little profit for the town, and the farmers and their kids love it."

I shrugged. "Guess I'll have to think about that for a while."

"Just let me know."

I nodded.

He said to his deputies, "You ride on ahead. I'll be right with you."

When they were gone, and he was keeping the reins tight so his big dun wouldn't bolt, he said, "She gonna break your heart, is she?"

"Looks that way."

"I used to keep score."

"Score?"

"Of how many times I got my heart broken." His gaunt, New England manner didn't look as if it would allow this kind of soft, female discussion.

I laughed. "Oh."

"Know how many times?"

"Guess not."

"Nine."

"That's a lot of pain."

Now he laughed. "But you know what?"

"What?"

"You always meet somebody else eventually. It just always happens."

"Maybe so."

"And you know something else?"

"What?"

"Sometimes they surprise you. Sometimes they go away and they come back."

When he said that, I felt a ridiculous hope that he was speaking of Evelyn and me, that she would indeed come back. Great, giddy optimism spread through me, and I felt that, at long last, my life was coming together, after all. Evelyn and I would somehow be together. Someday.

"That's nice of you to say."

"Give her a little time away," he said. "Don't be the kind of man that crowds her. Women don't like that."

Not much I could dispute there. "Thanks for all the good words."

He grinned. "Told you my pa was a preacher back in Kansas. Guess I got a little of the calling myself."

He touched the rim of his hat and rode away.

When I turned back to the asylum door, the huge stone

building looming castlelike above me, I saw the older man loading Evelyn's things into the back of the wagon.

As I passed him I said, "You want some help?"

He spoke into his beard and turned away. I could barely hear him. "No, thanks."

I nodded and went inside.

The optimism that Marshal Shay had put in me was still there.

I went upstairs to the apartment she'd been using, and just as I opened the door, I saw them there, the two of them, daughter and father.

He struck her hard across the mouth, so hard that he drew instant blood and jerked her head back viciously.

In less than three seconds, and with only one good arm, I was doing what I'd long wanted to do to the little bastard, pounding his head against the wall.

30

She had to pull me off him.

When my one good hand quit slapping him, he sank to the floor, touching his hand to his bloody mouth.

"You had no call—"

"I had plenty of call."

"Please, Mitch. I can handle him."

I touched my fingertip to the blood on the edge of her mouth. Again the temptation was to tell her that this man wasn't her real father. But I stopped myself once more.

Saunders got to his feet.

He went to the small window, looked down. "Your wagon's waitin'. If we're gonna finish our talk, we'd better do it now."

The room smelled close now, of sleep and grief, and I decided there wasn't much I could do here, after all.

"I'll be downstairs talking to the people in the cages," I said. "If you holler for me, I'll be able to hear you."

"I appreciate that, Mitch," Evelyn said, touching my arm.

I glowered at Saunders, hoping he'd be enough afraid of me to resist slapping Evelyn around anymore.

The folks in the cages got excited when I came back through. I went over to the middle-aged woman whose husband had hurt her so badly and said, "You won't have to worry about our friend with the whip anymore."

Hearing that, they started crowding around now, listening to me. I told them that Marshal Shay was going to have the man fired. I also promised them that he'd personally be responsible for the person who took the man's place.

"He won't hurt us no more?" an old man said.

"Not anymore."

He stuck a bony hand out through the bars and touched my shoulder. He had a sweet, sad old face. I tried not to notice his stench. It wasn't his fault, the poor old guy.

They saw her before I heard her. I followed their eyes, turning to see Evelyn coming quickly down the steps from her apartment.

"She's pretty," one of the women said.

Evelyn carried two small carpetbags, nothing else, walking without hesitation to the door to my right. Down the stairs, outside to the wagon, gone forever from my life.

Marshal Shay's optimism was already fading in me, like the last of an autumn day's sunlight. She was going now. Going for good.

"I'll help you," I said, catching up with her.

She shook her head. "Please, Mitch, after what I've just been through with my father—I just need to leave. I need time to think. And I'm already late."

This wasn't what I wanted here at the last, this exasperation. I wanted her to repeat what she'd said earlier, about us someday being together again. But I could see that this was the wrong time for such soothing words. Now there was just haste and anxiety, even a little anger.

"I love you, Evelyn," I said.

She kissed me again, up on tiptoes, eyes tight closed like a little girl giving an uncle a Christmas kiss.

Then she was footsteps down one, then two flights of stairs.

I heard the massive front door echo open and close, and then, through an open window on the second floor, I heard the sound of the wagon pulling away.

"Is she your girl?" one of the cage people asked me.

I smiled. "Hopefully."

Five minutes later I went down the same stairs Evelyn had taken a little earlier. I tried to smell her perfume lingering on the air but had no luck. The scent was just as gone as Evelyn herself was.

I was in a small alcove on the main floor, sipping coffee one of the matrons had handed me, when I saw Saunders walk past to the front door. He carried a familiar-looking pale blue eight-by-ten envelope under his arm.

"Well," the matron said. "We've certainly had an eventful night here."

"You sure have."

I sipped more coffee. I was tired and weak and facing a walk back to town. That was why I hadn't realized the significance of what I'd just seen. Not at first I hadn't.

I caught up with Saunders a few minutes later. He was walking down the winding, sandy road toward town.

"I didn't ask for no company."

"Oh, I'm not here for company, Saunders. I'm here to get a little truth out of you finally."

"You just leave me to hell alone."

We walked for a time. I enjoyed the cardinals and jays in the trees, and the cool shade beneath the pine boughs. I felt a part of nature, and it felt good.

He tried to walk ahead of me, but his legs were too stubby and his lungs too shot from cigarettes.

"That's a nice blue envelope you've got there."

"So? That blue envelope's my business. Just like everything else."

"She paid you again, didn't she? That's what you were

arguing about up back there. That's why you slapped her. Because she wouldn't pay you."

He didn't say anything.

He just tried to walk faster.

I grabbed his shoulder, spun him around, jerked the envelope from him.

Not easy, tearing it open with one hand, but I got it done while even managing to keep him from grabbing it back.

I whistled. "That's more than she paid you before. What secret are you supposed to keep now?"

"You leave me alone and give me my money back. You ain't got no right to that money at all."

He was so intensely fixed on his money that he didn't see me taking my Colt from my holster.

He didn't seem to notice it until I put it right smack against his forehead.

"Now, I want you to tell me why she gave you this money. And I want you to tell me now."

He heard it, or saw it, or sensed it, the fact that I was at the end of it all, all patience and probity gone.

I might just put a bullet in his forehead, after all.

He wasn't up for finding out.

"Tell me," I said. "Now."

He told me.

31

It took me fifteen minutes to get a horse and get it saddled, another five minutes to convince the matron that I really did need to borrow the carbine the absent doctor kept in his office, and then another half hour to find them.

He was still in disguise, a good enough disguise to fool me without any problem, looking every bit the unimportant asylum attendant Evelyn had told me he was.

They were just coming to the hill that led down to the small depot in the valley below.

I came up on the stage road beside them and smiled when I saw Evelyn.

"Thought you might have reconsidered. Thought maybe you wanted to come back."

She looked frantically at Steve Belden.

"But then again, Steve there probably wouldn't like that too much. You leaving him like that."

"I told you we couldn't trust that sonofabitchin' father of yours," Steve Belden said.

It hadn't been all that difficult. Buy off two of Marshal Shay's deputies, stage a jailbreak and shoot-out, and then have Steve, lying on the ground in front of the marshal's office, pretend to be dead. Pay off the undertaker and have him put Steve in the ground before anybody knows what's really going on, and Steve is ready to start a new life with a new identity. No more facing a hanging. No more living under the thumb of an overbearing father. And beautiful Evelyn is right in the middle of all of it, paying people off because she seems to be so afraid of Jeremiah and needing to get away from him.

"I want you to pull the horses over here," I said to Belden.

"We have money," he said.

"I'm sure you do."

"If you loved me, Mitch, if you really loved me, you'd let us go."

"Maybe. If you'd been honest with me. But it's a little late for that."

"You bastard," Belden said.

He'd always been fast, but against a one-armed man, he was even faster.

He shot me in my wounded shoulder before I could raise my gun and fire a shot.

Pain quickly became cold and blackness and panic. And then I felt myself slipping from my mount.

The ground was a lot harder than it needed to be, especially since I landed on my shoulder. But the additional pain gave me a quick burst of the energy only pure rage can fill you with.

I scrambled up on one knee, blinked my eyes until some of my vision came back, and sighted along my gun barrel.

The wagon was pulling on ahead, almost out of range, when Belden turned around and started to take a good clear shot at me.

Two things happened next, right at the same time.

I started to squeeze on the trigger, and Evelyn threw herself in front of Belden's gun, screaming, "Don't kill him, Steve! He's a good man!"

Well, I'm sure I don't have to tell you what happened next.

How Belden's shot, the one intended for me, the one that would likely have cost me my life as vulnerable as I was at the moment—how the shot went right into Evelyn's heart, throwing her backward from the wagon.

Now I didn't want my sight, didn't want to see Evelyn falling through the air and crashing, all broken and dead, on the rutted dusty road.

For Belden, I didn't matter anymore.

He got the horses stopped, jumped off the wagon and fell to his knees next to Evelyn.

He began sobbing immediately, and in a way I knew all too well, the way I'd sobbed all those long nights right after I'd shot and killed my son.

I got to my feet and staggered over to him.

"I killed her," he said, over and over and over. "I killed her."

And then he grabbed one leg of my pants and looked up at me and said, "Please kill me, Coldwell. Please don't let me live. I don't want to live. Honest to God, I don't!"

I couldn't enjoy it. I wanted to hate him, but I couldn't, because in a strange, sad way we were brothers now, having killed the people we most loved with our own hands.

There was no stopping his tears, I knew, so I just went over and sat beneath a tree and looked out at the vast valley so fiery and beautiful on this cool autumn day, and thought of how it made so little sense, these jokes that fate or the gods seem to play on us, these jokes that put at least a little bit of bitterness into every prayer we pray.

He got up once, still sobbing and loud and crazy, and started looking for his gun and shouting, "You fucker! You give me my fucking gun!"

But I wasn't about to give him his fucking gun because

I knew what he'd do with it. The same thing to himself he'd done to Evelyn, the same thing I'd done to my boy.

After a long, long time he fell into a bed of autumn leaves and slept.

By the time he woke up, a horseman had found us and had returned with two men from the depot below.

Epilogue

You remember me mentioning John Thomas Neville, the stage Englishman who does all the barking for The Belden Family Wild West Spectacular?

Well, like me, Neville decided to stay with the show after the city council took it over. Mainly because, again like me, he didn't really have anyplace else to go.

The council even fixed the show up a little, painted some of the signage, putting a pony ride for kids out back, and even gave us some new wild western costumes to wear.

Little by little the traces of Jeremiah Belden's days here are fading. There's even talk that the council will give the place a different name at some point, drop the Belden out altogether.

Unlikely as it sounds, Steve Belden wrote me a couple of times before he was to be hanged, telling me that he was glad I'd loved Evelyn, because she was truly a woman worthy of love. He didn't have anybody else to write to, he said, and hoped I didn't mind the letters he kept sending me. Between the lines you could sense all his panic and pain, which explains, I suppose, why he hanged himself in his cell three weeks before the state was supposed to do it for him.

* * *

Yesterday was kind of a bad day for me, a warm April Saturday, because there was this family that wanted to have its photograph taken with me in my new western outfit.

Oh, I didn't mind the picture so much. It was mostly the boy who gave me trouble. He looked so much like Mac, my own son, that after they left, I went into a darkened tent that nobody was using and cried.

Last night, at supper, I told Sonia Eckstrom about it and she came over to me right at the table there, and held me a long, long time, even started crying some herself.

Then afterward we had our usual talk, about how she hopes that someday I'll love her as she loves me, as I once loved Evelyn. And how she hopes that I'll also give up liquor entirely, someday.

I sure hope so, too; I sure do.

THE DEVIL'S DANCE FLOOR

by

Gordon D. Shirreffs

Dave Hunter and Ash Mawson, U.S. Army
scouts, are searching for renegade Apaches in
the Arizona Territory. When a priceless fig-
urine of the Virgin Mary is stolen, Dave and
Ash find themselves on a wild and dangerous
quest for the thieves. And many bullets will
fly before justice is served.

This exciting adventure set in the Old West is
coming to your local bookstore in
March 1994.

Published by Fawcett Books.